Desire, Unexpected And Unwanted, Slammed Into Shane With The Force Of A Runaway Train.

As if a veil had been ripped away, he saw her with absolute clarity. No longer was she an uncertain youngster, an awkward adolescent, the sweet but gawky little sister of his best friend. Instead, she was a woman in every sense of the word, from the full curve of her breasts to the dip of her slender waist to the length of her Vegas-showgirl legs.

Shane's world seemed to tilt. He suddenly wondered who the hell he thought he'd been kidding.

His libido hadn't sprung back to life for no reason.

It was her. *Jessy*. God help him, but he wanted her....

Dear Reader,

The perfect treat for cool autumn days are nights curled up with a warm, toasty Silhouette Desire novel!

So, be prepared to get swept away by superstar Rebecca Brandewyne's MAN OF THE MONTH, *The Lioness Tamer,* a story of a magnetic corporate giant who takes on a *real* challenge—taming a wild virginal beauty. THE RULEBREAKERS, talented author Leanne Banks's miniseries about three undeniably sexy hunks—a millionaire, a bad boy, a protector—continues with *The Lone Rider Takes a Bride,* when an irresistible rebel introduces passion to a straight-and-narrow lady…and she unexpectedly introduces him to everlasting love. *The Paternity Factor* by Caroline Cross tells the poignant story of a woman who proves her secret love for a brooding man by caring for the baby she *thinks* is his.

Also this month, Desire launches OUTLAW HEARTS, a brand-new miniseries by Cindy Gerard about strong-minded outlaw brothers who can't stop love from stealing their own hearts, in *The Outlaw's Wife.* Maureen Child's gripping miniseries, THE BACHELOR BATTALION, brings readers another sensual, emotional read with *The Non-Commissioned Baby.* And Silhouette has discovered another fantastic talent in debut author Shirley Rogers, one of our WOMEN TO WATCH, with her adorable *Cowboys, Babies and Shotgun Vows.*

Once again, Silhouette Desire offers unforgettable romance by some of the most beloved and gifted authors in the genre. Don't forget to come back next month for more happily-ever-afters!

Regards,

Joan Marlow Golan
Senoir Editor, Silhouette Desire

Please address questions and book requests to:
Silhouette Reader Service
U.S.: 3010 Walden Ave., P.O. Box 1325, Buffalo, NY 14269
Canadian: P.O. Box 609, Fort Erie, Ont. L2A 5X3

CAROLINE CROSS
THE PATERNITY FACTOR

SILHOUETTE *Desire*®

Published by Silhouette Books

America's Publisher of Contemporary Romance

SILHOUETTE BOOKS

ISBN 0-373-76173-2

THE PATERNITY FACTOR

Printed in U.S.A.

Books by Caroline Cross

Silhouette Desire

Dangerous #810
Rafferty's Angel #851
Truth or Dare #910
Operation Mommy #939
Gavin's Child #1013
The Baby Blizzard #1079
The Notorious Groom #1143
The Paternity Factor #1173

CAROLINE CROSS

always loved to read, but it wasn't until she discovered the romance genre that she felt compelled to write, fascinated by the chance to explore the positive power of love in people's lives. Nominated for a number of awards, including the Romance Writers of America's prestigious RITA Award, she's been thrilled to win the *Romantic Times* Reviewer's Choice Award for Best Desire, as well as a W.I.S.H. Award. She grew up in central Washington State, attended the University of Puget Sound and now lives outside Seattle, where she (tries to) work at home despite the chaos created by two telephone-addicted daughters and a husband with a fondness for home improvement projects. Caroline would love to hear from her readers. She can be reached at P.O. Box 5845, Bellevue, Washington, 98006.

To Lyle and Janice, with love and thanks for all these
years of friendship and support.
I got lucky when they were handing out in-laws.

One

"**I** mean it, darling. What you need is one good woman."

"Thanks for the suggestion, Mom," Shane Wyatt said dryly. "If you knew how much I used to hope you'd say something like that when I was a teenager..."

Jessy Ross, cloaked in the shadow of the eaves as she swayed slowly back and forth on the porch swing, smiled. She knew she shouldn't eavesdrop, but she couldn't resist—that last comment was pure, vintage Shane.

Her amusement faded, however, as she continued to listen to the pair leaning against the deck railing. Although their backs were to her, their voices carried clearly on the light summer breeze.

"You can joke all you want, Shane, but this isn't a laughing matter. With your father and me leaving for

Minnesota next week, and not getting back until September, Chloe is going to need someone.''

''And like I told you yesterday,'' Shane replied, ''I've been checking out a new day care and lining up extra baby-sitters—''

''Which is precisely the problem.'' A note of asperity crept into Helen Wyatt's voice. ''Chloe is only two, darling. She needs some continuity in her life, not a constantly changing roster of caregivers. I know you mean well, but I really think you need to consider finding someone to move in with you for the summer.'' Helen's voice suddenly softened. ''I know it's only been eighteen months since the accident, and it might feel strange at first to have a woman other than Marissa in the house, but for Chloe's sake...''

There was a moment of dead silence; even from her vantage point Jessy could see that Shane's big body had gone tight with tension. She watched as he rolled his shoulders, then rammed a hand through his thick black hair, obviously struggling for patience.

''Look, Mom,'' he said finally. ''I'll think about it, okay? But it's not as easy as you make it sound. Finding someone that both Chloe and I like, who doesn't mind the isolation out at the lake... It's just not that easy,'' he repeated, his voice strained.

Jessy took a deep breath, peripherally aware of a number of things: snatches of conversation from the backyard party going on around them; the utterly trusting way little Chloe lay sleeping in her arms; the lingering aroma of charcoal-broiled steak wafting from the barbecue grill; the warmth of the June sun as it hovered above the western horizon.

More immediate was the sudden acceleration of her heartbeat as she heard herself say, ''I could do it.''

For a moment, nothing happened. Then mother and son spun around, their expressions a study in contrasts as they caught sight of her sitting there. In a matter of seconds, Mrs. Wyatt's face went from surprise to dawning delight.

Shane's, on the other hand, was starkly unenthusiastic. "Jessy?" Beneath straight black eyebrows, his pewter eyes were cool. "I didn't realize you were there."

Refusing to be daunted, she returned his stare. Although his features were the ones she'd always known— the straight, strong nose, the angular cheekbones, the stubborn chin—he didn't look at all like the man she'd adored as a teenager. There was no amusement lighting those densely lashed eyes, no laughter lurking at the edges of that chiseled mouth. "I'm sorry. I didn't mean to startle you," she said evenly. "I probably should have said something when you first walked up, but I didn't want to wake Chloe."

His gaze dropped to her lap, a flicker of surprise— and something vaguely unsettling that she couldn't identify—crossing his face as he belatedly noticed his daughter.

"I really didn't mean to eavesdrop," she added.

To her relief, Helen Wyatt finally found her voice. "Don't be ridiculous, dear. You were obviously here first. Besides, it isn't important. What matters is what you said about taking care of Chloe. Did you mean it?"

"Of course she didn't, Mom," Shane said flatly. "I'm sure Jess has better things to do with her summer than baby-sit for me. She's probably got plans to hang out, see her friends, work on her tan. Right, Jess?"

He made it sound as if she were a sixth-grade student instead of a sixth-grade teacher, Jessy thought with a touch of exasperation. Yet even so, for a moment as their

eyes met, she felt herself transported back to a time
when she'd been twelve and he'd been twenty and she
would have done anything to please him.

Then Chloe gave a faint little sigh and shifted closer,
her small body warm and boneless, and Jessy was
abruptly brought back to the present. Even if his wife's
death hadn't changed Shane, it had been a long time
since the days when Jessy had been madly in love with
her brother Bailey's best friend. Despite what Shane
seemed to think, she was no longer an awkward, im-
pressionable adolescent. She was a grown woman of
twenty-six who knew her own mind and who—thanks
to him—had learned to trust her instincts.

And what her instincts were telling her, and had been
for some time, was that something was terribly wrong
in Shane's life, something more than the normal grief of
losing his wife, as bad as that was. Jessy couldn't imagine what it could be, wasn't even sure she was right, but
if there was even the slightest chance she was, she
wanted to help.

Before she had a chance to say so, Chloe stirred again,
as if disturbed by the adults' tension, and slowly opened
her big blue eyes. She stared uncertainly up at Jessy and
popped her thumb into her mouth.

"Hey, sweetie." Jessy smoothed a springy golden
curl behind one of the little girl's shell-like ears. "Did
you have a nice nap?"

The toddler nodded, then looked around, a tentative
smile lighting her pixielike face when she caught sight
of Shane. Extracting her thumb from her mouth, she
struggled into a sitting position. "Dada?" she said hope-
fully, raising her arms to her father. "Get uppie?"

For an instant Shane didn't seem to hear. Then he

abruptly stirred to life. Stepping forward, he bent down and scooped the child up.

Jessy didn't miss either that telltale hesitation or the faint shadow that darkened his face as Chloe gave a little sigh of pleasure and locked her arms around his neck. Although both reactions were gone in a flash, they were a further confirmation of all the niggling little misgivings that had been plaguing her for months.

It was one thing for Shane to erect a wall between himself and his friends and family. It was quite another for him to rebuff his own child, no matter how inadvertently.

The realization strengthened her newfound resolve. Enough that she didn't hesitate when Helen cleared her throat and said, "Well, Jessy? What do you say? *Do* you have plans for the summer?"

Jessy forced her gaze away from Shane and his daughter. "No, I don't. I meant it when I said I'd love to look after Chloe. And actually Shane would be doing me a favor. The condo I rent has just been sold, so this would give me a chance to take my time finding a new place. Better yet—" she leaned forward and smiled reassuringly at Chloe, who was clutching her father's T-shirt in one small hand "—I think we'd have fun, wouldn't we, pumpkin?"

The toddler nodded solemnly.

"It's settled then!" Helen said brightly. She looked up at Shane. "Isn't that wonderful, darling?"

Shane's face looked carved from granite. "Wonderful."

Ignoring his less than eager response, his mother gave him a cheery pat on the shoulder, then turned back to Jessy. "So, dear. How soon can you move in?"

* * *

Shane couldn't believe it. He was thirty-four years old, the founder and CEO of TopLine Sports, a sporting equipment company that employed more than a hundred people and would make a multimillion-dollar profit this year alone. He owned his own home, he voted and paid taxes, he'd been married and widowed.

Yet as he stood in his front hall Sunday afternoon and watched through the screen door as Jessy Ross pulled her little red car into his driveway, he had to admit he was no match for his mother. She'd beat him fair and square a week ago when she'd pounced on Jessy's baby-sitting offer and made it into a fait accompli.

That wasn't why he was going along, however. He was doing this because his mother was right. Chloe did need more stability in her life. She'd been a secure, happy seven-month-old at the time she lost her mother. Now, a year and a half later, after two different day cares and at least a dozen different evening and weekend baby-sitters, she was often clingy and too quiet.

Yeah? And whose fault is that?

Shane's mouth flattened out as guilt, familiar and irksome, plucked at him. Stubbornly he tried to ignore it; after all, it wasn't his fault he had to work—or that there were certain...*truths*...he couldn't seem to forget. Besides, it served no purpose. Bottom line, Chloe needed someone she could depend on, and though Jessy was only a temporary answer since she would go back to her teaching job in the fall, her stay would at least give him time to find someone permanent.

It wasn't going to be easy having someone in the house, though. Sometimes he thought the only thing that had kept him sane the preceding year and a half had been his absolute insistence on his privacy.

He took a firm grip on his thoughts. The past was

over and done. It had taken him a long time to work through feelings, to get past the grief and the rage that had nearly consumed him. Now that he'd finally reached a blessed state of indifference, he wasn't about to jeopardize it by getting all worked up about this or anything else.

Besides, if he had to have his solitude invaded, there was a measure of comfort in familiarity. And Jessy was certainly that, he thought, observing her as she climbed out of her car. Like her older brother, she was tall, with cornflower blue eyes and the kind of skin that turned gold with just a little sun. Unlike Bailey, however, who was a gifted athlete with the sort of looks and laid-back charm that attracted the opposite sex the way honeysuckle drew bees, Jess had been a shy, gawky kid who'd worn braces and been prone to tripping over her long, skinny legs.

Now, dressed in a navy T-shirt and khaki shorts, with her straight, honey-colored hair caught up in a ponytail threaded through the back of a Mariner's baseball cap, she looked the way she always had—leggy, boyish, unpretentious. Shane supposed if he had to have a female around, he should be grateful it was her. At least he didn't have to worry about an unwanted attraction.

He watched as she reached into her car. Despite the distance, he could see the thing was packed to the roof with stuff. He sighed; she always had been a bit of a pack rat. When she emerged, however, the only thing she held was a gift-wrapped package. Nudging the door shut with one slim hip, she took a leisurely look around, her gaze sweeping slowly over his contemporary, single-story house. Even as he told himself she couldn't possibly see him, standing as he was in the shadows, her gaze locked right on him.

"Shane!" She tucked the package under one arm and started toward him. Faster than he would have believed possible, given her lazy, loose-limbed gait, she was suddenly standing on the other side of the door. "Hi." Her gaze searched his face, and for a moment her blue eyes seemed slightly wary. Then she smiled. "Well? Are you going to ask me in?"

"I see you found the place." He pushed open the screen.

She stepped past him into the cool, dim hall. "Yes. Your mom gives good directions."

"She should. She's been telling people where to go for years."

The corners of her wide, full mouth quirked despite his sour tone. She looked around. "This is nice. How long have you—" she hesitated for a second as she glanced to her right into the sunken living room, which was, like the dining room beyond it, completely devoid of furniture "—lived here?"

He let loose of the door. Ignoring the questions he could see in her eyes, he started down the hall toward the combination family room-kitchen, gesturing for her to follow. "A year."

"Ah."

In sharp contrast to the hallway, the back of the house was bright with sunlight. Narrowing his eyes against the sudden glare, Shane headed for the breakfast bar, expecting Jessy to follow.

Instead she stopped a few feet inside the room to stare at the view beyond the trio of sliding glass doors that opened onto the big cedar deck. "Wow. I didn't realize you were actually on the water. From the front of the house, you'd never guess. How beautiful."

He glanced out indifferently, looking past the wide

expanse of emerald lawn that ran down to the shores of
Lake Winston. The lake's tranquil waters sparkled in the
afternoon sunlight, while in the distance the snow-tipped
peaks of the Cascades stood sentinel against a powder
blue sky.

He shrugged. "It's all right."

Again, her eyes sought his. But before he could identify the look in hers—sympathy? concern? distress?—
she glanced away. Stung, and not sure why, he wondered
caustically what her reaction would be if he told her that
at the time he'd bought the place, he'd simply been looking for something that didn't remind him of Marissa.

Crossing his arms, he watched her examine the ultra-
modern black-and-white kitchen that occupied the area
to their right, then check out the long, curved breakfast
bar with its six chrome-and-leather swivel stools. Next,
she switched her gaze to the family room area, which
boasted a cathedral ceiling, a pale wood floor and a big
stone fireplace. Although not lavishly furnished, it did
have a fully functional entertainment center and an oversize black-and-white sectional sofa.

Her expression lightened as she caught sight of Chloe,
who was sitting quietly on the floor in front of the TV,
watching *Beauty and the Beast* on video. "Hey, Chloe.
How're you?"

The toddler glanced over. For a moment she looked
uncertain, the way she so often did. Then she saw who
it was and her face creased with a bashful smile.
"Jeddy." Clambering to her feet, she abandoned Walt
Disney and toddled over to the end of the sofa, where
her nerve suddenly ran out. She ducked her head and
shyly regarded Jessy through her lashes.

"Guess what, sweetie?" Closing the distance between
them in a few unhurried strides, Jessy sat down on the

sofa, then lifted Chloe up and gently plunked the child down beside her. "I brought something for you. A present."

The child's eyes widened with surprise. "Fo' me?"

"That's right." She laid the package in the little girl's lap.

"Oh." Chloe started to reach for the bright pink bow, then suddenly stopped. She looked up at Shane. "'Kay?"

Shane nodded, feeling the usual combination of guilt and helplessness at the little girl's diffidence.

Reassured, she turned her attention back to the package. Biting her bottom lip with concentration, she carefully pulled off the bow, making a little sound of surprise when Jessy took it and stuck it on her head. She reached up to touch it, gave a quiet giggle, then went back to work, tearing at the paper. Suddenly her big blue eyes and her Cupid's bow mouth both rounded. *"Ohhh,"* she said reverently, staring at the small, soft-bodied doll. *"Baby."*

"I didn't have a clue what she had for toys," Jessy said softly to Shane as she took the baby doll out of its box and handed it to Chloe, "but I figured she could always use another doll."

Shane shrugged, not about to admit that up until a moment ago he'd believed two was still too young for such things. "It's fine," he said gruffly, watching as the child very carefully touched one small finger to the doll's closed eyes.

"Baby sleeping," Chloe said solemnly.

Jessy turned her gaze back to the child. "Yes. Unless…" She tipped the doll upright, rewarded as its eyes fluttered open, prompting the child to give a little gasp.

"Ohh! Pwetty."

Jessy's face softened and she gave the toddler a gentle hug. "Yes, but not as pretty as you. What are you going to call her?"

For once, Chloe didn't hesitate. Lifting her chin she said clearly, "Belle."

"Mmm." Jessy directed an amused look at the TV, then glanced over at him. "Figures," she said conspiratorially.

Shane tensed. Not only didn't he have the first idea what she was referring to, but for a second there, as he watched her warm, spontaneous interaction with Chloe, he'd been suddenly, starkly reminded of just what it was he'd lost.

Irritated—just what the hell was wrong with him?— he paced over to the window, struggling to get a grip on himself.

"Shane? Is everything okay?"

The quiet question jerked him around. "Yeah, of course," he said brusquely. "I was just thinking there are some things we need to discuss."

"Okay." Settling deeper into the sofa, she crossed one long, slim leg over the other and waited.

He pushed away the last remnant of unwanted emotion and forced himself to concentrate. "First, what days do you want off?"

She looked surprised. "Gosh, I don't know. I just got here. Can't we play it by ear?"

He shook his head. "No. I need to know so I can make other arrangements."

She bit her lip thoughtfully. "Well… Why don't you plan on me taking care of Chloe at least through next weekend to start with, then? That way you don't have to worry about making other plans, and I'll have some time to see how things go. We can discuss it again after I have a better idea of what's involved.''

Shane didn't like it, but he could see her point. "All right.''

"Good." She smiled. "What else?''

"Your salary. I'm not sure what you have in mind, but I thought maybe…twenty-five hundred a month?''

Her eyes widened. "You're kidding.''

"Make it three thousand, then.''

She made a low sound of protest and shook her head. "Shane—no.''

"No what?''

"Just…no. I appreciate the offer, but my teaching job pays me more than adequately during the summer. Besides, you're doing *me* a favor, remember? Thanks to you, I've got a few months to look for a place to live.''

He stared at her earnest face, then realized he should have expected this. Jessy always had been a quixotic, kindhearted kid. She was the sort of person who cried over old movies, worried about stray puppies, championed the oppressed and defended the downtrodden. It was just like her to selflessly donate her time to an old family friend.

Except that he didn't want her help—much less these little ripples of feeling she kept causing in him.

Yeah? Well, you're not doing this for you, remember? You're doing it for Chloe, so she can have some of the emotional security you're incapable of giving her.

That didn't mean he had to be here, however.

The realization brought him up short. He thought about it for a handful of seconds, then came to a sudden decision. "All right," he said abruptly. "If that's the way you feel." Why argue about money? He'd simply decide on a sum and give it to her later. No doubt she'd be more inclined to take it once the reality of the situation caught up with her good intentions.

Besides, he was now anxious to move on to other things. "Look. Why don't I show you where the phone list and the emergency kit are, then you can see your room and the rest of the house. That way I can help you get your car unloaded before I have to go."

Jessy's surprise was obvious. "You're leaving?"

"Yeah. I need to go into the office for a few hours."

"Oh." She gave him an indecipherable look, then slowly nodded. "I see. All right." She stood and held out her arms to Chloe. "Come on, cupcake. You can keep us company while your daddy shows me around, okay?"

The toddler hesitated, clutching her doll to her chest. "Baby, too?"

Jessy nodded. "Baby, too."

Chloe still didn't move. Then, apparently suffering a belated attack of shyness, she scooted off the couch, scampered over to Shane and pressed herself against his legs. "Want Dada," she mumbled.

"Chlo—" Shane remonstrated.

The little girl buried her face against his knees, refusing to look at either adult.

Shane stared down at her small blond head. Part of him wanted to lift her up and hold her tight, to breathe in her sweet baby scent and assure her that Daddy was there and everything was going to be all right.

And part of him wanted to step away.

"It's all right," Jessy said, misunderstanding. "Really."

But it wasn't. It was never going to be all right again, he thought savagely, clenching his jaw against a jab of self-disgust. Totally out of patience with himself, he reached down and swung Chloe up, settling her securely in the crook of one arm. "It's okay, peanut," he murmured. Raising his voice, he looked over at Jessy and said coolly, "I guess we're ready."

She nodded, but the questioning look he was already starting to hate was back in her eyes. "Okay."

He glanced away. He was just tired, he told himself. He'd go to the office for a few hours, come home and get some sleep and tomorrow, or the next day, when the strangeness of the situation had worn off, he'd have himself back under control.

Not that it mattered. Because the truth was, he'd gladly give up his control, this house, even TopLine itself, if he could only go back to the time before he'd learned Chloe wasn't his daughter.

Two

"Elvis," Jessy murmured as she stood at the front window and watched Shane's car pull out of the driveway, "has left the building." She glanced at her wristwatch, struggling against a sense of disbelief.

It was a little after five o'clock, not quite three hours since she'd arrived.

She asked herself what she'd expected. That Shane would stick around, maybe keep an eye on Chloe while she unpacked? That they'd sit down to some sort of dinner and talk—about his schedule, about who was going to tackle which housekeeping tasks, about Chloe's wants, needs, likes and dislikes, fears and foibles?

Or, better yet, that he'd suddenly break down and confess he was glad she was there?

Well... Yeah.

The admission prompted a slight, self-deprecating smile. *Get a grip, Jessica. You volunteered to do this, remember? It certainly wasn't Shane's idea. And if his behavior is any indication, he isn't exactly overcome with joy at having you join his household.*

Of course, now that she'd seen the house in question, she could understand his reticence.

She turned, giving a theatrical shiver as she surveyed the living and dining rooms. Like the rest of the interior, they were done predominantly in white—carpeting, walls, woodwork and blinds. Also like the rest of the interior, they had high ceilings and windows that were strategically located to maximize the various views of the surrounding woods and lake.

Jessy could see that the place had potential. Yet all that white, plus the absolute lack of such personal objects as artwork, keepsakes or photographs—not to mention such fundamentals as furniture—made it about as cozy as a glacier. She supposed she was biased, accustomed as she was to the clutter, color and organized chaos of her classroom, but to her mind it was definitely not the sort of warm, homey place best suited to raising a child.

But then, from what she could tell, Shane wasn't exactly trying to get himself voted Father of the Year, she reminded herself as she padded across the living room and stepped into the hall.

Jessy shook her head and admitted she didn't understand it. Not from Shane, who'd been the rock her own childhood had been built on.

After her mother had walked out on them, she, Bailey and their dad had relocated from Denver to Churchill, which at the time had been just another small town outside of Seattle. For Jessy, the move had meant the loss of everything dear and familiar: her home, school and friends, her grandparents and her cousins. Even worse, her father had been extremely bitter about the desertion. He'd shut everyone out and buried himself in his new job, too caught up in his own feelings to pay much attention to anyone else's.

Bailey, on the other hand, had acted as if nothing had happened—except that he would walk away from the conversation anytime their mom was mentioned. At seventeen, he'd put all his energy into building a new life at his new school with his new friends, and because he was smart, athletic and exceedingly handsome, he'd been almost immediately accepted. That had left Jessy all by herself—bereft, bewildered and lonesome.

She'd heard about Shane for weeks before she finally met him. He'd been Bailey's new best friend, so she'd known he was captain of the football team and student body president, that he made straight A's and dated only the prettiest, most popular girls. He'd sounded so perfect, she'd been fairly sure she wouldn't like him. Not that it would matter. If he was anything like the rest of her brother's friends, he probably wouldn't even notice that she existed.

Still, as luck would have it, their first meeting took place following her most disastrous day at school ever. She'd failed her math test, lost her book report, then gone without lunch because her dad had again forgotten to go to the grocery store. Things hadn't gotten any better when Bailey had failed to pick her up after school the way he was supposed to, either. The class bully had pushed her in a mud puddle on her way home, causing her to skin her knees and tear her favorite dress. And as if that weren't bad enough, when she finally did make it home, she'd found her brother was entertaining half the football team, while a note from her dad had said he wouldn't be home until late.

It had been too much. Too proud to cry in front of a bunch of teenage boys, she'd made it as far as the big tree in their backyard before she'd sunk to the ground and let the tears overwhelm her. It hadn't been pretty. She'd cried until her eyes were puffy, her throat was raw and her nose was runny.

The latter had become a definite problem once the worst of the emotional storm had passed. Hiccuping painfully, she'd been lamenting her lack of a sleeve when a beautifully timbered voice had said softly, "Here. Take this."

Her eyes had flown open and she'd found herself staring at a wad of fresh tissues, held by a handsome stranger with soot black hair and the kindest, most beautiful gray eyes she'd ever seen.

For a moment all she could do was stare at him. Then, miserably aware he must think she was the biggest baby ever, she'd mumbled a thank-you, taken the tissue and carefully blown her nose, refusing to meet his gaze. Instead she'd just sat there, too mortified to do or say anything.

To her surprise, after a moment he'd sat down beside her, his hard, warm shoulder touching hers as if they'd known each other forever. "Tough day, huh?"

She'd nodded, swallowing around the fresh lump in her throat at the unexpected sympathy in his voice.

"You must be Jessy," he'd said. "I'm Shane. One of Bailey's friends."

"Oh," she'd said stupidly.

He hadn't seemed to notice that in addition to being a crybaby, she was also a moron. Instead he'd leaned back on his hands, nodded in the direction of her raw knees and said casually, "So...is there somebody you want me to beat up for you?"

She'd been so stunned by the offer she'd forgotten her swollen eyes and red nose and turned to look at him. "You'd do that for me?"

He'd shrugged, and her heart had felt a little lighter as she'd seen the sudden spark of laughter in his eyes. "Sure. I don't have a little sister of my own. It would be my pleasure."

That had been the start of an unlikely friendship that had sustained her through the next ten years. One way or another, Shane had always been there when she needed him. When she'd tripped and broken her wrist at sixth-grade graduation, he'd been the one who'd kept her company while the doctor set the fracture. When she'd gotten braces and grown five inches freshman year, it had been Shane who'd assured her she wasn't a freak. He'd taught her how to play pool, shoot a basket and cheat at poker. He'd listened when she needed to talk about her mother, and shown up with the world's hokiest horror movie when she didn't have a date for the prom. He'd brought laughter and security back to her life and she'd adored him for it.

Like the naive child she was, she'd thought he would be there for her forever. In some romantic, unrealistic part of her mind, she'd believed she and Shane were destined to be together, that he'd wait for her until she grew up. So even though she'd known he was dating Marissa Larson, a petite, ultrafeminine blonde who was everything she wasn't, she'd been totally devastated when Shane had announced his engagement ten days before she was scheduled to leave for college.

She could smile about it now, but it had taken her a considerable amount of time to put it in perspective and accept that her love for Shane had been a childhood kind of thing. She shook her head, remembering.

Still, it didn't really matter. Whatever name she put on what she'd felt for him in the past—true love, childish crush, teen idolization—it didn't change the fact that she considered him one of the best friends she'd ever had.

Or that this was her chance to pay him back for all the years he'd stood by her.

She reentered the family room, where Chloe was once again parked in front of the TV set watching a video. All alone, with her thumb in her mouth and her long silky lashes looking like miniature fans every time she blinked, she was the picture of defenseless innocence. Jessy slowed her pace, startled by the strength of the protective urge that swept through her at the sight of that sweet little face.

A sudden sense of purpose filled her. Shane might have taken off, but Chloe was here—and definitely in need of an adult she could count on. Making her voice light and cheerful, she said, "Hey, sweetie. I was thinking. It's a beautiful day out." She approached the child and tried to look reassuring. "How would you like to go for a walk before dinner?"

The toddler glanced over, appeared to consider, then said uncertainly, "'Kay."

"It'll be fun," Jessy promised. "We can take some bread and see if we can't find some ducks to feed down at the lake."

The child perked up, climbing to her feet with a sudden look of interest. "Duckies go *quack-quack*."

"Yes, they do." Jessy ejected the video, turned everything off and held out her hand. "You're pretty smart, aren't you?"

Chloe hesitated, then took a few steps and tentatively

laid her soft little hand in Jessy's. Looking up through her lashes, she nodded.

Jessy's heart melted, while her resolve hardened. *Don't worry, baby. One way or another, whether he likes it or not, I'm going to chase those shadows from your daddy's eyes.* After all, as Shane himself had taught her, that was what friends were for.

She smiled down at his daughter. "Come on, kiddo. We're going to have some fun. I promise."

"Good morning," Jessy said cheerfully.

She watched with distinct satisfaction as Shane rocked to a halt in the doorway that led from the hall into the kitchen. In the split second before his expression smoothed out, his dismay at finding her already up at such an early hour was obvious.

His lack of composure didn't last long. "Good morning," he returned brusquely. Resplendent in a crisp white shirt and a beautifully cut gray linen suit that set off his inky hair and his olive-toned skin to perfection, he came the rest of the way into the room. He set the morning newspaper on the breakfast bar. "What are you doing up?"

She gave a little shrug. "I heard you come in from your run, and since I was wide-awake, I decided I might as well get up and put the coffee on."

"Huh." He pulled out a stool, sat and opened the newspaper, effectively dismissing her.

So what else was new? she asked herself, struck once again by the immense change in him. It had been after midnight when he finally came home that first night, and he'd been gone again before seven the next morning, a pattern that had repeated itself in the three days since. Except for a photocopy of his schedule that he left her each morning, Jessy's chief contact with him was by phone. As if to prove he wasn't completely irresponsible, he called every day to ask how things were going.

She swallowed a rude sound and turned to watch the coffee as it slowly filled the pot. Although she hadn't expected him to suddenly decide he was overjoyed by her presence, neither had she expected him to avoid his own home as if it were infested by the plague just because she was in it.

But he had. He was. And she'd had enough. After three days of thinking about it, she'd decided it was time to get tough.

In the nicest possible way, of course.

The coffeepot gave a last sputter, indicating it was done. She looked over at Shane. "The coffee's ready. Would you like a cup?"

He was silent a moment, then glanced up. "Sure."

She got a mug from the cupboard, filled it with coffee, added some creamer and set it down beside him.

"Thanks." He went back to the paper.

"You're welcome." She took a moment to study him, taking in the firm line of his freshly shaven jaw, the inky blackness of his thick eyelashes, the latent sensuality of his mouth.

He shifted, raising the paper higher and she glanced away, feeling the oddest little ache. Giving herself a mental shake—what was that all about?—she crossed to the other counter and went back to the batter she'd been putting together when he walked in. She checked the recipe, added the last few ingredients, then picked up the bowl and a wire whisk and began to stir. After a few moments, she turned. Resting her backside against the counter, she glanced at Shane. "I hate to bother you," she lied, "but I have a favor to ask."

"Yeah? What?"

Although she couldn't see anything except his hands and the top of his dark head, she sensed his sudden tension. "Well...I wondered if you'd mind if I got my table and chairs out of storage and brought them over. It's not that I don't like eating at the counter," she explained. "It's just that it's the wrong height for Chloe's high chair and meals would be so much easier if—"

"Jessy." The paper came down and he regarded her impatiently. "You want a table? Fine. Call Robinson's. Tell them to send something out and have them put it on my account."

He had an account at the furniture store? She bit her lip, resisting an impish urge to ask him why, if that was the case, the house was emptier than a pauper's wallet. While the old Shane would have come back with a smart remark of his own, she was pretty sure the new one would stiffen up like a starched sheet hung out in a hot breeze, and she wasn't quite done with him yet.

"Really?"

"Really."

"Would it also be all right to get one of those rocker-recliners so I'd have someplace to read to Chloe?"

"Get whatever you want," he said flatly.

"Okay. Great. I'll do that."

"Good." As quickly as that, the paper went back up.

Thoughtfully she set the bowl down on the counter, got the margarine out of the fridge and the syrup out of the cupboard. She poured the latter into a measuring cup, then checked the light on the waffle iron, which indicated it wasn't quite ready. Picking up her coffee mug, she once more faced the breakfast bar. "Shane?"

"What?"

"There's something else I'd like to ask." She smothered a smile as she heard him sigh a second before he lowered the paper again.

One straight black eyebrow slashed up in question. "What is it now?"

"How would you feel about painting Chloe's room?"

He frowned. "What's the matter with it the way it is now?"

"It's just so...bland. I'd like to add some color, maybe do a wallpaper border, just...brighten things up. Make it more suitable for a small child."

For a moment he looked as if he were going to balk. Just as quickly, however, his face smoothed out, returning to its usual indifferent mask. "Fine. Pick out the paint and I'll get somebody in to do it."

"Don't be silly," she protested. "I'll take care of it. I like to paint."

He shrugged. "Do whatever you want."

She smiled at him sweetly. "Great. I'll do it Saturday then—if you're free to watch Chloe?"

His expression grew even more shuttered. "Sure." He started to go back to the paper, then reconsidered. "Is there anything else?"

"Well... As a matter of fact..."

"What?"

"Would you like some breakfast?"

He shook his head. "No, thanks. I'm not hungry."

"Oh. Okay."

With a rustle of newspaper, he returned to the day's headlines.

Jessy didn't say a word. On the contrary, she turned serenely around, set down her mug, flipped up the top of the waffle iron and poured in a puddle of batter. She replaced the top, picked up the syrup and put it in the microwave to warm.

In seconds the kitchen was filled with tantalizing aromas.

She pretended not to notice, just as she continued to ignore Shane. Instead she set a place for herself at the counter, poured herself a glass of milk and placed it, the margarine and the now-warm syrup within reach. Then she retrieved her waffle, put it on a plate and sat down. Settling her napkin in her lap, she picked up her knife and carefully buttered the warm, golden circle.

Two stools down, Shane had gone very still.

She reached for the syrup and slowly drizzled it across the waffle's steaming surface. Then she cut off a bite-size piece and popped it into her mouth, unable to completely mask a soft sigh of pleasure at its sweet, buttery taste.

Very slowly, the paper came down. "You didn't tell me you were fixing waffles," Shane said brusquely.

"You didn't ask."

"I didn't think I had a waffle iron."

"You don't. You were a little shy on cookware, so I brought over some of my things."

He gave her a long, indecipherable look, then deliberately laid down the paper, pushed back the stool and stood. "I've got to go," he said curtly. He stalked out of the room.

"Have a nice day," Jessy called after him. She calmly ate another bite, thinking it was too bad he was so pressed for time.

Waffles were his favorites.

Three

When Shane walked in the door after work Friday night, Jessy was curled up on the family room couch, reading a magazine.

She sat upright as he came into the room. Pushing her glossy mane of golden brown hair off her face, she sent him her usual friendly smile. "Hi."

He tossed his keys onto the counter and loosened his tie with a jerk. "Hi, yourself."

He realized he sounded surly, but he didn't particularly care. The whole damn day had been horrible. He'd overslept and missed his morning run. The rain that had threatened for two days had commenced at exactly the same time he'd had a tire blow out on the freeway. When he finally arrived at the office, damp, disheveled and late for an important meeting, he'd learned that Grace, his secretary for the past three years, had fallen in the shower and broken both arms. Topping things off, a shipment meant for Minnesota had gone to Missouri, one of his major suppliers was having financial problems and the truckers' union was making noise about a possible strike.

Now here he was, home at last. Or at least, he *thought* it was his home, he amended, taking a swift look around. In the time since he'd left that morning, it appeared he'd acquired an oversize rocker-recliner, several occasional tables, a pair of table lamps and a richly patterned Persian rug for his family room, plus a sleek dinette set that now occupied a space next to the windows.

Following his gaze, Jessy said mildly, "The furniture came."

"Yeah. I noticed." He was in no mood for small talk. It was after eight, he had indigestion from the too-spicy pizza he'd eaten for dinner and he was dead-dog tired. All he wanted was to be left alone, to have a little quiet time to get his head together before the whole damn thing started all over again in the morning. Not that he expected her to care.

"You're home late." She drew up her legs and looped her arms around them.

"Yeah." He'd gone by the hospital to take Grace some flowers and wound up spending more than an hour assuring her she didn't have to worry about her job, the hospital bill, or anything else. "I guess I should have called."

"No problem," she said easily. "Have you had dinner?"

"Yeah." He picked up the mail and began to sort through it.

She was silent a moment. "Tough day?"

"You could say that."

"I'm sorry. It must be the rain. Chloe had a bad one,

too, poor little thing. It wore her out. She was out like a light by seven-thirty.''

He set down the mail, which except for an invitation to one of his best customer's wedding was mostly flyers and bills, and turned to face her. "Well, I'm not far behind her. I'm going to go for a short run, then turn in, okay?''

It wasn't a question so much as a declaration of his need for space, but she nodded anyway, her eyes very blue in her tranquil face. "Fine by me. I'm going to finish this article and then watch a movie. Enjoy your run.'' That said, she curled up, propped her head on one hand and went back to her magazine.

Shane remained where he was for a second, feeling off-kilter and not liking it. Turning on his heel, he started out of the room, only to grind to a halt halfway across the floor. Exasperated with himself, he slowly retraced his steps. "Listen,'' he said without preamble, certain that the next few minutes were going to be about as pleasant as the rest of his day. "I almost forgot. I have to fly to Dallas tomorrow. One of my suppliers is having some cash flow problems. Can you handle things with Chloe?''

Jessy looked up, studied his face for all of two seconds and said, "Sure. Don't worry about it.'' She resumed reading.

He stared at her finely drawn profile. That was it? No muss, no fuss, no major upset? "Okay then,'' he said, feeling inexplicably irritated.

She nodded but didn't look up, and after a moment he turned and left the room, his annoyance growing with every step. He stopped briefly to look in on Chloe—the kid was flat on her back and snoring noisily—then changed out of his suit and into some sweats, and went for his run.

It was still light out, so he started out on the wide, well-maintained path that circled the lake. Later, he'd take one of the many offshoots and come back along the road to the house, but for now the wide vista of silvery water suited his mood.

For the first mile or two he tried not to think. He concentrated instead on the even ebb and flow of his breathing, the cool slide of the rain against his skin, the firm feel of the running path beneath his sneakered feet.

At some point, however, he began to brood about his exchange with Jessy. What was her problem, anyway? Why did she have to be so damn accommodating? It wasn't normal—not for a female. She was so rational, so reasonable, so calm and sensible. She acted just like a guy.

Only she wasn't a guy, he reminded himself impatiently. She was Jessy, the motherless little buddy he'd practically adopted back in high school. And for all her lack of pretension, her penchant for dressing in T-shirts and shorts, for going without makeup and wearing her hair simply, there had always been a kindness about her, a sensitivity to other people's feelings, that was markedly feminine. So, too, was the way she'd always looked up to him, treating him as if he were some sort of paragon or, better yet, her own personal knight in shining armor who could do no wrong.

Shane grimaced. Now, that was a laugh. A real man wouldn't care that the child he loved wasn't truly his. He'd be able to get past his wife's betrayal, to get on with his life instead of merely going through the motions—

He clamped down on his thoughts, his stomach twisting with the familiar self-disgust. He'd been over this ground so often he knew every futile twist and turn, every useless bump and bend. No matter how often he considered it, or how much he wished things were different, that *he* could be different, it changed nothing.

Nor did it help to address the situation with Jessy. As much as he hated to admit it, all the time he'd been telling himself she'd be good for Chloe, part of him had nevertheless been dreading the moment when she finally saw him for the sorry son of a bitch he really was.

Yet so far—despite his less-than-admirable demeanor—she'd been nothing but warm and understanding. And she'd saved him a monumental hassle tonight when she'd agreed to stay with Chloe while he went to Dallas. Without her, he'd be back at the house calling childcare agencies, not out in the fresh air running off the day's worries.

He considered the rest of the week. He had to concede that because of her he'd been able to come and go as he liked, instead of juggling sitters. And she was certainly easier to deal with than his mother, who had recently started nagging him about the way he was neglecting her granddaughter. Best of all, it seemed that he could trust Jess not to demand more than he was able to give.

He reluctantly conceded he ought to be grateful for her presence. But had he shown even the slightest appreciation? Hell no. Instead, ever since she'd moved in, he'd been expecting her to act like Marissa. He'd been waiting for her to demand his attention, to complain that he was never home, to sulk or pout or cry.

But she hadn't—for which he was damn grateful.

He sighed. Under the circumstances, he supposed it wouldn't kill him to act a little more civil. He could still keep his distance. It didn't mean he had to spend any time with her or let down his guard.

For some reason, the decision lifted his spirits. He picked up his pace, pounding out the next few hundred yards, then slowed as he approached the house. By the time he'd showered and thrown on a T-shirt and jeans, he felt nominally better.

It wasn't until he came down the hall to put his dirty clothes in the utility room that he heard the opening theme from *Star Wars*. Surprised, he stopped in the doorway, sure he must be mistaken until he glanced across the room and saw the opening credits unrolling on the TV screen. He was swept by a wave of nostalgia; the George Lucas saga had been his absolute favorite as a teenager.

He wasn't sure how long he stood there before he admitted he was hooked. He edged into the room and watched for a while longer, then set down his laundry, walked over and finally sat gingerly down in his new recliner. He felt Jessy glance over at him briefly, but she didn't say anything.

During a lull in the action, he cleared his throat. "Jess?"

"Hmm?"

"Thanks for staying with Chloe this weekend."

It was a moment before she spoke. "No problem. You want some popcorn?"

"Sure."

As she passed him the bowl and he realized that was the end of it, something inside of him that had been wound tight began to uncoil just a little.

"Oh, I almost forgot," she said suddenly. "Bailey called. He said he'd give you a call in the office next week."

"Yeah?" Although not as close as they'd once been, he and Jessy's brother still talked periodically. In addition to their friendship, Bailey had an endorsement contract with TopLine, thanks to his status as one of the NFL's premier quarterbacks. As usual for this time of year, he was at summer camp with the rest of the Florida Falcons. "How's he holding up?"

Jessy's teeth flashed briefly in the dim light. "He sounded beat. He says the younger players have been giving him a pretty hard time. I think he finally means it about this being his last season."

"Maybe." Shane put up the recliner's foot rest and leaned back. "Although what he's going to do afterward…" His voice trailed off as his gaze met Jessy's. There was no need to say more, since they both knew how tied to football Bailey's identity was—and how difficult it was going to be for him when he finally gave it up.

"He'll be all right," Jessy said firmly. Her face suddenly lit with a quick, impish grin. "Everyone has to grow up sometime. Even Bailey."

To his surprise, Shane started to smile back, then abruptly caught himself. He forced himself to speak coolly. "Yeah, I suppose." After all, he didn't want to give her the wrong impression; he might be glad for her help with Chloe, appreciative of her easy-going manner, even impressed with her insight when it came to Bailey, but that was it.

Just as he was no longer the person she remembered, their youthful camaraderie was also over, and the sooner she accepted that, the better off they'd both be.

Yet even as he turned his attention to the movie and forced himself to concentrate on a galaxy far, far away, he couldn't stop the errant thought that if he had to have somebody around, he could have done a whole lot worse than Jessy Ross.

"Dada!"

Shane lifted his suitcase out of the Explorer's trunk. Setting it on the driveway next to his briefcase, he twisted around at the sound of Chloe's voice, surprised to see her emerge from the jogging path that led to the lake. She raced forward, her chubby little legs churning, and launched herself at him.

Short of letting her crash to the ground, he had no choice but to sweep her up and into his arms. Yet he'd no more lifted her up than he found he had a whole new problem as she promptly wrapped her arms around his neck in a stranglehold. "Hey, Chlo, take it easy," he said, his voice muffled against her silky head.

Her response was to press a noisy kiss to his ear. He tensed, uncomfortable with the display of affection, only to have his attention diverted as a familiar feminine voice said wryly, "I think she missed you."

He looked up and found Jessy standing at the edge of the pathway. For some reason, the sight of her gently amused face seemed to lessen the strain of the moment. "Yeah, I guess."

She resumed walking, her long legs eating up the handful of yards between them as she crossed the narrow strip of lawn. Dressed in a pair of white shorts and a cocoa-colored tank top that brought out the gold tones in her hair and skin, she looked strong and healthy and vibrant. "Welcome home."

"Thanks."

"How did it go?"

He shrugged. "Okay." He gave Chloe a cursory pat, then reached up and unsuccessfully tried to unpeel her arms from his neck. Swallowing a sigh, he settled on shifting her sideways, awkwardly holding her in the curve of one arm so he could reach down and grab his suitcase with the other.

When he straightened, he found Jessy watching him, her expression thoughtful. Catching him by surprise, she leaned close and laid her hand gently on Chloe's back. "Hey, sweetie. Why don't you show Daddy what you have?"

For a few seconds the toddler didn't react. Then, to his relief, she suddenly raised her head and let loose of his neck. Leaning back, she unexpectedly held up a water-filled plastic bag she had clutched in one small hand. "Isa goadpish, Dada," she said.

He glanced from the bag, where a skinny little orange fish was doing its best to navigate the swirling, Chloe-induced currents, to her earnest little face and back again. "Nice."

She looked excessively pleased. "Wudy gibbed it to me. Wudy has lotsa goadpishes."

He looked inquiringly over at Jessy.

"Rudy Markovich," she clarified, leaning over and picking up his briefcase. She started toward the front door and it seemed the most natural thing in the world to fall into step beside her. "He lives on the point—the big gray Colonial with the flag. He's retired and into fish. Mostly tropical, but he also has a goldfish pond."

He considered the healthy flush in her smooth cheeks. "I take it you guys have been for a walk?"

"That's right."

Leave it to Jessy to go for a stroll and wind up making a friend. With his luck, she'd be on a first-name basis with the entire neighborhood by the end of the summer, ruining any chance of totally reclaiming his privacy once she was gone.

Yet as he glanced down at Chloe's glowing face, he had to admit his irritation suddenly seemed petty. Besides, what could he do? Ask Jessy to stay in the house with the blinds closed?

He could imagine her reaction to that.

With a caustic twist to his mouth, he murmured his thanks as she opened the door for him and they proceeded inside, continuing on into the living area after he'd set his suitcase in the hall.

He paused in the doorway, struck by how different the room looked. Part of it was due to the new furniture, no doubt. But there was also no denying that Jessy's presence had brought an infusion of life and color to the place.

A fuzzy pink pastel baby blanket was draped over the back of the couch; a jumble of red, blue and green blocks were piled next to the entertainment center, and there was a pair of women's sandals lying in front of a sliding glass door. There were three brilliantly hued fingerpaintings taped to the refrigerator; a half-dozen pillows in rainbow colors piled across one end of the couch, and a child's yellow plastic pail sat on one end of the breakfast bar, filled to overflowing with a bouquet of summer flowers in crimson, maroon and magenta.

The lived-in look didn't end there, either. Out on his formerly pristine deck, there was now a pair of patio chairs with electric blue cushions, a matching chaise longue and a bright turquoise wading pool. A trio of rubber ducks bobbed on the pool's shallow surface, as did a hot pink beach ball, while a pair of red-and-white beach towels that had been tossed over the rail gently flapped in the breeze.

It looked like a home. And it smelled like one, too, thanks to the rich, tantalizing scent of roast beef that was wafting from the oven. Against his better judgment, he heard himself say, "Something smells good."

Jessy gave a dismissive little shrug. "Pot roast."

He glanced at her sharply. Like waffles and *Star Wars,* pot roast was one of his favorites and he was struck by the sudden thought that she was deliberately trying to please him. For an instant he felt uneasy, wondering what she wanted from him, and then he caught himself. After all, this was Jessy—not Marissa.

She headed into the kitchen. "So, were you able to get things straightened out with your supplier?"

"Yeah." He turned to keep her in sight. "Things are still shaky, but we managed to come up with some interim financing."

"That's good." She began to search through the cupboards. Finally finding what she wanted, she went up on tiptoe and lifted down a heavy glass bowl. He frowned as he found himself thinking that she wasn't quite as skinny as he remembered.

She started toward the sink, only to hesitate as she glanced over and found him staring at her. "Shane? Is something wrong?"

He jerked his gaze from her fanny to her face. What the hell was wrong with him? he wondered impatiently. "No. No, I just—where'd that come from?" Hoping he didn't sound as lame as he felt, he indicated the bowl.

"Oh. It's mine." She turned on the tap and rinsed it out, then filled it with water and set it on the counter. "Chloe, sweetie, why don't you come with me—" she walked around the end of the counter to where he stood and held out her arms "—and we'll put your fishie in his new home."

"'Kay."

She leaned in and he handed her the toddler. For a moment before the transfer was complete, he could feel the soft pressure of her hand as it grazed his chest, and smell her light scent, a pleasing combination of soap and carnations.

She straightened and walked away. He stared after her. For a few disconcerting seconds there, he could have sworn he'd felt something that bore an alarming resemblance to...awareness.

Which was absolutely ridiculous. After all, this was Jessy he was talking about. Jessy, who was practically one of the guys, whom he'd known since she was nine, who—although her effort was misguided—was just trying to make his life a little easier by being here.

He must be more tired than he'd thought, he decided. Either that or he was just plain mistaken, and had simply confused a belated appreciation for her warmth and kindness toward Chloe for something more elemental.

Yeah. That must be it. Because thanks to what Marissa had done, he didn't want to be aware of anybody. And even if he changed his mind in the future, the last person he'd consider would be Jess, who was too young and too naive to be expected to cope with the kind of baggage he carried.

At the counter, she helped Chloe lay the bag on the water, floating the fish the way that was proper. "There. Mr. Fish should be ready to go in the water after dinner." She glanced over at him. "Have you eaten?"

"No."

"Good. Right after I clean up a certain person—" she tapped Chloe on her button nose "—I'll fix the salad and then we'll eat."

He shook his head. "You two go ahead. I'm going to

shower and change first.'' Mistaken or not, he saw no reason to push it.

''No problem,'' she said pleasantly. ''We'll wait. The truth is, I'd really appreciate the company. As much as I like the munchkin here—'' she glanced affectionately at Chloe, then flashed him an apologetic smile ''—I've had about all the baby talk at meals I can handle. I'd really like to hear about what's going on in the outside world.''

He stared at her. Despite her light tone, there was the slightest note of strain in her face and he suddenly felt ashamed. Here she'd taken care of Chloe for nine days without a word of complaint, and he was too selfish to even stick around for a meal. ''All right. Thanks. I won't be long.'' He headed for the hall.

''Hey, Shane?''

''What?''

''I'm glad you're home.''

Remembering the vow he'd made four days ago to try to cut her some slack, he said gruffly, ''Yeah. So am I.''

It wasn't the truth, of course.

Yet for the first time in a long time, it wasn't quite a lie, either.

Four

"Want wadey pool," Chloe said plaintively.

"I know, sweetie." Jessy slid the last batch of chocolate chip cookies into the oven. She straightened, then glanced over at the little girl who was standing at the sliding glass door, with her nose pressed against the glass, staring wistfully out at the inflatable pool Jessy had bought her. "I'll take you out just as soon as the cookies are done. I promise."

Chloe shook her head. "Want wadey pool," she repeated, her little face the picture of entreaty.

"You don't want to go out there now," Jessy said patiently. "Daddy's still mowing the lawn. It's too noisy."

As if to prove her point, Shane came striding up the slight slope from the lake, the steady hum of the lawn mower growing louder the closer he came to the house. The afternoon sunlight glittered on his ebony hair, while large patches of sweat dampened his pale gray T-shirt, molding it to the muscled planes of his chest and stomach.

"Jeddy?"

"Hmm?" She dragged her gaze away from Shane, perplexed as the hollow feeling that had plagued her off and on lately returned to the pit of her stomach. She must have eaten one too many dollops of cookie dough, she decided, as she met Chloe's pleading gaze.

"Want wadey pool. Pwease?"

"In a little while, cupcake," she said, even though she knew darn well it wouldn't help. If there was one thing the past two weeks had taught her, it was that two-year-olds had no sense of time, didn't know what waiting meant, and that sweet, shy little Chloe could be absolutely relentless when she wanted something. True to her fairylike looks, the child didn't cry or pitch fits; she simply repeated what she wanted, over and over again.

It was, Jessy thought wryly, the toddler equivalent of Chinese water torture. *Drip, drip, drip,* and pretty soon you were reduced to a quivering heap who would do anything for a few minutes of peace and quiet.

"Pwease, Jeddy?"

Her only hope was distraction. "Tell you what. Why don't you take Belle and see if you can find her swimsuit? I think it's in your room, in your toy basket. That way she can go with you in the pool when it's time."

The child's eyes lit up. "Belle wim, too?"

"Yep. Belle can swim, too. But first she has to get out of her clothes and into her swimsuit like you."

"'Kay!" Chloe took off like a shot, clearly happy to have something to do.

Jessy picked up the spatula and began transferring the

cookies she'd already baked from a sheet of wax paper on the counter to a plate.

Things were looking up, she thought happily. Not only did she have a moment to herself, but Shane was actually home for a change. She had to admit that his gruff announcement that he planned to be around for most of the weekend, made while they were watching the second *Star Wars* movie last night, had caught her by surprise. But it was a good kind of surprise—as was the recent improvement in his manner.

Ever since his return from Dallas, he'd seemed a little more forthcoming, a little more at ease, a lot less tense. Jessy wasn't sure whether he'd simply become resigned to her presence or if he was actually beginning to accept that she was going to be his friend no matter what he said or did, but she was certainly relieved. For a while there she'd begun to think she was kidding herself by thinking she could improve his situation.

She gave a start as the buzzer on the oven rang, jolting her from her reverie. She turned it off, picked up a hot pad and opened the oven. The room seemed oddly quiet until it dawned on her that she could no longer hear the lawn mower. Shane must be done, she decided, setting the cookie sheet on top of the stove.

Her assumption was confirmed a minute later when he walked past the window directly in front of her, opened the sliding door and came inside. She turned to keep him in sight as he headed for the utility room. "All done?"

"Yeah." Stripping off his T-shirt as he went, he used it to scrub his face and neck, which were slick with perspiration. Then he wadded it up, opened the utility room door and lobbed it in the general direction of the washer and dryer with one powerful flick of his wrist.

That dratted hollow feeling was back again. Vexed, she turned around, picked up the spatula and began to transfer the warm cookies onto the wax paper, wondering what on earth was the matter with her.

"Damned if it isn't hot out there." Shane walked over, got a glass and crossed to the sink, which was directly to her left. He flipped on the water. "I'm parched."

"At least it's not raining," Jessy said lightly. The fragrance of fresh-cut grass clung to him, mixing pleasantly with the clean, musky scent of the sweat on his skin.

He made a low sound of agreement, then gulped the entire glassful of water. He refilled it and drank again, this time more slowly. Setting the glass on the counter, he reached across her and stole a handful of cookies.

Jessy reacted instinctively. Having grown up with Bailey, who would eat an entire batch of cookies all at once if you let him, she turned and rapped Shane on the shoulder with the spatula. "One at a time, please."

"Ow!" He recoiled in surprise.

Abruptly she realized what she'd done. "Oh, dear," she said, trying hard to sound apologetic although she thought it was rather funny. "I'm sorry. I suppose I shouldn't have done that."

One straight black eyebrow rose. "No kidding. I guess I'll forgive you, though." A faint smile tugged crookedly at his mouth. "I'd forgotten how quick your reflexes are."

Relieved, she reached up to brush off the cookie crumbs the spatula had left on him. "Living with Bailey, I had lots of practice. I didn't hurt you, did I?"

The smile widened into a sardonic grin. "I think I'll live."

His skin was toast warm and velvet soft. She looked

at his smiling face, drinking in the sight of the slight dimple in one tan cheek, the whiteness of his teeth and the way the skin crinkled around his eyes, and suddenly everything changed. To her shock, desire snuck up out of nowhere and scorched her like a thief with a blowtorch. Flustered, she snatched her hand from his shoulder, tore her gaze from his face—and found herself looking straight at his bare chest.

She told herself to look away.

She couldn't. Instead, in a single moment that seemed to go on forever, she took the measure of his broad shoulders and hard stomach, then found the time to follow the path of the silky wedge of jet black hair that started at his collarbone, narrowed to an inky stripe at the bottom of his pectorals and plunged like an ebony arrow straight to his shallow navel before disappearing into his low-riding jeans.

Her nipples puckered, while the vague little ache in her stomach migrated south—and was no longer vague at all. She wanted to step closer, stroke that silky line of hair with her fingers, feel the pulse beating at the base of his throat with her mouth—

"Jess?"

She jerked as if he'd goosed her. "What!"

"Is something the matter?"

"No!" Her heart pounding, she lifted her gaze and apprehensively searched his face, certain he must know what she was feeling. To her utter and total relief, however, his expression was mildly curious and nothing else.

"Are you sure?"

"Yes, of course." She forced herself to take a calming breath. "I'm sorry. I'm afraid my mind was wandering."

Uh-huh. From your pecs to your navel and under your shorts...

Chloe, bless her heart, chose that moment to reenter the room. Desperate to put some distance between herself and Shane, Jessy set the spatula on the counter and turned her attention to the child. "Hi, sweetie! Did you finally find your dolly?"

"Uh-huh." The little girl held up Belle triumphantly. She'd managed to strip the clothes off the doll, which was now naked except for the bright orange nylon swimsuit dangling precariously from one plastic arm. "Go wadey pool now?"

"You betcha." Jessy aimed an apologetic smile in Shane's direction and walked swiftly into the family room. "We'll just grab some sunblock and towels, and then it's into the water for the two of you." She scooped up the doll-toting toddler, causing Chloe to give a little shriek of delight. "As for *you*..." She took a calming breath, plastered what she prayed was a noncarnal look on her face and forced herself to turn around, knowing it would look odd if she didn't say something to Shane. "Don't eat all the cookies."

Totally oblivious to how sexy he suddenly looked to her, he crossed his arms and leaned back against the counter. "I'll think about it. But I'm not making any promises."

She swallowed, sharply aware of the irony. Just as he was starting to let down his guard and lighten up, her libido was threatening to sabotage everything.

Yet even knowing it was so didn't help. Her gaze flicked from the lock of raven hair that tumbled over his forehead, to that killer chest, to the way his jeans were molded to his narrow hips and long legs. Her whole body clenched.

She managed a nod and fled.

* * *

Shane sighed with satisfaction as he stood beneath the cool spray of the shower.

It had been an okay day, he reflected, running his fingers through his hair to remove the last traces of shampoo. Quiet, but okay. In addition to mowing the lawn, he'd washed his car, swept the garage, paid some bills and remembered to send in the RSVP. for the Martinson wedding. Hell, he'd even taken a nap for a change.

Not that anything was really different, he was quick to remind himself. Spending one day at home, puttering around, didn't mean a thing. Still, it was nice to take some time off, to get away from the office and just kick back. And there had been a few times during the day, such as his and Jessy's cookie encounter, when he'd actually been able to forget the past. It was strange, but for a little while, he'd felt almost at peace.

He shut off the water. Stepping out onto the thick white rug, he toweled dry, tossed his running clothes into the hamper and padded into the oversize bedroom. Although starkly furnished with a king-size bed, a nightstand and lamp, a massive black lacquer bureau and a single upholstered chair, it was saved from austerity by a glassed-in wall with wide French doors that revealed a sweeping view of the lake.

He walked across to the bureau, pulled out a clean T-shirt and jeans and proceeded to dress. He felt a mild sense of anticipation, and realized he was looking forward to watching the final *Star Wars* movie tonight. Which just went to prove how really dull his life had become, he thought ruefully as he walked down the hall and into the family room.

Not surprisingly, his attention was claimed by Jessy and Chloe, who were curled up together in the recliner reading. Maybe it was his mellow mood, but for a moment as he considered them he felt a flash of something almost like tenderness. It didn't take long for the more acerbic side of his nature to reassert itself, however.

"Hey, Jess?"

"Hmm?"

"You can quit reading now."

She looked up from the book in her hands. "I can?"

"Yeah." His voice was dry. "Chloe's asleep."

"Oh." She glanced from him to her young charge, her gaze lingering on the little girl's parted lips and closed eyes. "I guess she is."

He felt a tug of affection for Jess. She was dressed casually in a light blue tank top and navy shorts, idly rocking the recliner with one bare foot as she sat with Chloe cradled sideways on her lap. With her long bare legs and her hair caught up in a single braid, she didn't look a day over seventeen.

"Well," she said, laying the book on the floor next to the chair, then shifting Chloe in preparation of climbing to her feet. "I'd better get her to bed then."

Shane allowed himself a slight frown. Although it was subtle, she seemed a little subdued and sort of jittery. But then, she'd done an awful lot today, baking cookies, doing laundry, taking Chloe to the lake to feed the ducks, fixing yet another excellent dinner. She was probably just tired. Being the good sport that she was, however, she'd never ask for help, much less complain.

Without making a conscious decision, he found himself closing the distance between them. "Here." He stopped in front of the chair. "I'll take her."

"That's all right—"

"No. I'll do it." Steeling himself, he leaned over and slid one hand along her thigh in order to get his arm under Chloe's narrow shoulders. Jessy jumped a little at the contact and he glanced sideways at her. "Still ticklish, huh?"

She nodded, a faint flush rising in her cheeks.

He felt a tic of amusement, the way he had earlier that day in the kitchen. "Relax," he advised her. "This'll only take a second." He bent closer, slipped his free hand between the soft upper swell of her chest and the child, took a firm hold on Chloe and straightened. To his surprise, he felt the slightest bit breathless. He shook it off and stepped back. "There."

"Thanks." Jessy climbed to her feet.

"No problem." Hefting the toddler higher, he balanced her limp weight against his chest and waited as Jess gathered up Chloe's doll and blanket, then followed her down the hall to the baby's bedroom.

The blinds were already drawn; the room was cool and shadowy. Shane carefully laid the child in her crib, watching as she stuck her thumb into her mouth and rolled to her side with a contented little sigh.

For some reason, he found himself reminded of the day she'd been born. Despite everything that had happened, he hadn't forgotten how he'd felt: excited, anxious, awed—and then, the instant he saw her red, wrinkly, precious little face, profoundly, irrevocably, in love.

And he still loved her, he thought with a combination of tenderness and despair. Even though he couldn't forget that day in the pediatrician's office, right before her first birthday, when he'd seen the innocent little notation in her chart regarding her blood type that had changed his life forever.

After the initial shock had worn off, and the confirming tests had been done, he'd found himself caught in a depth of despair so enormous it dwarfed everything that had come before. He'd grieved for his lost paternity, his identity as a father, his idealized marriage, his shattered trust—and he'd done it alone, unwilling to reveal his humiliation, unable to share his pain.

His grief had been so profound, he might not have survived—except for the rage that ultimately supplanted it. But as the days had passed, he'd become consumed with anger. He'd been angry at Fate and the cruel trick she had played on him. He'd been furious with Marissa, desperate to know why and with whom she'd betrayed him, while bitterly aware that he'd never know the answers. And last, but far from least, he'd raged at himself, despising his own gullibility and his failure to see the truth.

He'd sold his house, and everything in it. He'd limited his contact with friends and family. He'd kept to himself, finding salvation in work, and eventually a blessed sort of indifference had set in.

Only lately, even that feeling seemed to be changing. Yet as long as it was just with Jessy, he supposed it was all right. After all, they were buddies.

"She's really out," Jessy said quietly, leaning over and covering Chloe with a thin blanket, then placing the child's doll at the head of the mattress.

"She had a busy day," Shane replied, putting the past from his mind. He glanced at the clean line of Jessy's profile. "So did you."

She gave a slight shrug as she straightened. "I didn't do that much."

"Yeah, you did."

"No. I didn't. Now shh." She pressed a finger to her lips and dredged up a quick smile before heading out of the room.

He followed her into the hallway, closed the door behind him, then reached out and caught her by the arm. "Hey, hold on a second, Jess."

She stiffened at his touch and swung around so quickly, he almost ran her down. "What?"

"I just—is there anything you need? Anything I can do for you?"

"No. Of course not," she said, but not before an odd look crossed her face. "Why do you ask?"

He lifted one shoulder. "I don't know. You seem sort of…jumpy. And the thing is, if you'd like some time off, or for me to hire a cook or a cleaning lady—"

"I'm fine, Shane."

He raised an eyebrow, allowing his doubt to show. "Are you sure?"

"Yes. I suppose I'm a little tired, but a good night's sleep and I'll be back to normal." She hesitated, then added with determined cheerfulness, "As a matter of fact, I thought I'd paint Chloe's room tomorrow—if that's okay with you?"

He relaxed at the confirmation that his earlier surmise had been right. "Sure. I'll help."

"Oh, no! You don't have to—"

"I know that. I want to."

"But what about Chloe? Somebody has to watch her."

"We can do it during her nap. I've got to go into the office for an hour or two in the morning, so it should work out fine."

"Oh," she said, sounding rather uncertain. "If you're sure."

It was just like her not to want to impose on him, he thought fondly. "Yeah, I am."

"Okay then." She took a sideways step in the direction of her room. "Well…good night."

Shane looked at her curiously. Deciding to ignore the fact that it was only a little after eight, he said instead, "Aren't we going to watch the movie?"

She stopped, looking sheepish. "The movie. Of course. I forgot."

He could see the slight strain in her face. Ignoring a twinge of disappointment, he said, "Look, if you're too tired, let's skip it. We can do it another time."

She hesitated, then came to a decision. "No. Don't be silly. It's too early to go to bed anyway."

"Great." Shane followed her down the hall, not speaking again until they were at the doorway.

"Hey, Jess?"

"What?"

"I just want you to know…you're a really good friend."

There was a moment's silence before she answered. "Thanks."

Feeling more upbeat than he had in a long time, he went to put in the movie.

Five

There was nothing like painting to help vent your frustrations, Jessy told herself, energetically working the roller up and down Chloe's wall.

Not that she was frustrated. She wasn't.

Annoyed was more like it. Every time she thought about how she'd behaved with Shane the previous day, she felt like an idiot. And it irritated her.

First, there had been that lunacy in the kitchen, when she'd acted as if she'd never seen a man's bare chest. Heck, she'd acted as if she'd never seen *Shane's* chest before. But she had. She'd seen it dozens and dozens of times over the years. Yet for some reason she'd chosen yesterday to get all tongue-tied and goggle-eyed.

Of course, that was no worse than the way she'd reacted to his help putting Chloe to bed last night. She'd practically gone up in flames in response to his inadvertent touches. And then, when they'd been out in the hall and he'd asked if she needed anything, she'd actually been tempted to say, "Well, as a matter of fact, I need to touch you—all over. And I want you to touch me, too."

As for the movie... Suffice it to say she'd had a tough time concentrating, thanks to an awareness of Shane that had been all-consuming. Heck, for all she knew, Darth Vader and the Dark Side might have triumphed over Luke and Hans and the Force.

Jessy sighed, wondering again what on earth had gotten into her. If she didn't know better, she'd almost think she was still carrying a torch for Shane.

She wasn't. Sure, he was great-looking, in an utterly masculine way she'd be the first to admit was devastating. And yes, he could be mesmerizing when he chose to employ a little charm, the way he had yesterday. And okay, she did seem to spend an inordinate amount of her time thinking about him. Heaven help her, last night he'd even cropped up in her dreams, half naked and hot to the touch, his eyes intent and his hands sure and knowing—

Stop it, she told herself crossly. *None of that means anything.* She was *not* attracted to him. It was the situation that was getting to her, the fact that they were living in such close quarters. That, and the way she'd been thinking so much about the past, remembering how things had been and how she used to feel about him.

Besides, it certainly wasn't as if Shane were thinking about *her* in any sort of erotic or libidinous way. He'd made that perfectly clear when he'd told her what a good friend she was.

Even as she winced at the recollection, she told herself she ought to be grateful that at least he didn't have a clue about her recent bout of lust.

She forced herself to focus on the here and now. Chloe's room was coming along, she thought staunchly, taking a look around. She'd moved the child's crib into the spare bedroom, and moved everything else—the dresser, changing table and an oversize rocking horse—into the center of the large, square room, covering them with plastic. She was applying a warm, sunny shade of blue on the walls, a nice complement to the white carpet, woodwork and louvered closet doors. In a few days she'd put up the cheerful yellow, white and blue wallpaper border she and Chloe had picked out and some shelves for the child's toys.

She hoped Shane liked it. Because she planned on being done with the painting by the time he got back from the office, and she was counting on him being so grateful he'd readily agree to stay with Chloe while she went to run some errands. It wasn't that she wanted to avoid him, exactly. It was more that she needed some time alone, to put things in perspective. She was confident that with a little time and a minimum of distance this mistaken sense of attraction she felt for him would disappear, becoming nothing more than a mildly amusing memory—

"Jessy? What the hell do you think you're doing?"

The unexpected sound of Shane's voice made her jump. She spun around and clapped a hand to her chest as she found him standing in the doorway not two feet away. "Good grief! What are you trying to do? Give me heart failure?"

"I should be so lucky," he murmured, sounding distressingly like the Shane of old. "Now, answer the question."

She pursed her lips, really, really hating it when he

talked to her as though she were five years old. "What does it look like? I'm painting."

"I can see that. The question is, why? I told you I'd help as soon as I got home."

She shrugged, since she certainly couldn't tell him the truth. Not when she was dressed in a plain white T-shirt and her oldest short-alls, while he stood there, looking gorgeous in loafers and khakis and a pale yellow shirt. And not when the mere sight of him was again making her stomach hollow, her pulse race and the rest of her feel warm and tingly and strange.

She turned back to the wall and resumed painting, partly to underscore what she was about to say, but mostly to avoid looking at him. "Chloe went down early for her nap." It had only taken half an hour of fervent encouragement and the promise of an ice-cream cone after lunch to get the child to try to go to sleep. "So I decided I might as well get started. I have some other things I need to take care of today."

"I see." His tone made it clear he didn't. "Well, give me a minute to get changed and I'll help you finish."

"That's okay. I'm almost done." It was the truth; she had only a little of the last wall left to do.

There was a brief silence. "Yeah. I guess you are."

She glanced over and gave him a quick smile. "Thanks anyway, though." *Now go away.*

His expression thoughtful, he crossed his arms and leaned one broad shoulder against the doorjamb. "You missed a spot."

"No, I didn't."

"Yeah, you did." His teeth flashed whitely. "Trust a female to rush the job."

She pursed her lips. Why, why, after two weeks, did he have to choose now to be his old self? And where was his usual rush to leave when she could really use it?

"See? Right there." He pointed to a section of wall she'd finished some minutes ago.

She glanced briefly toward where he indicated. "I don't see anything."

"Oh, for Pete's sake." He made a chiding sound as he stepped into the room and walked gingerly across the plastic tarp to the place he'd indicated. "Not only inefficient, but oblivious, too." Stopping beside her, he pointed downward. "Right there."

Afterward, she wasn't sure what the devil made her do it. Maybe it was his proximity. Maybe she was worn-out from too much thinking and too little sleep. Maybe it was his persistence or his confounded teasing.

Or maybe it was the aggravating sight, proving him right, of a quarter-inch strip of white showing near the taped-off baseboard.

Whatever the reason, as she reached to take care of the bare spot, her hand seemed to take on a life of its own. As quick as the proverbial arrow, it swooped over and painted a bright blue swath down the front of his shirt.

"What the hell—" Shane dropped his chin to get a better view of himself, then glanced back up, looking stunned. "I can't believe you just did that."

Neither could she. Yet now that it was done, she couldn't seem to stop either. With a flick of her wrist, she reversed course and ran the roller over his face. "There," she said recklessly, thinking that if this didn't make him leave, nothing would. "You look just like Mel Gibson in *Braveheart*."

His gaze bore into her, his slate gray eyes unreadable in a sea of azure.

"Well, okay, maybe not exactly," she conceded nervously, ignoring the strident little voice asking if she'd lost her mind. "But you are the right shade of blue."

"Oh, really?" His eyes gleaming dangerously, he reached down, yanked his shirttail free and very deliberately wiped off his face. "Well unfortunately for you—" he suddenly snatched the offending roller out of her hand "—I happen to be one of those people who always has to see things for himself."

It didn't take a genius to guess what was coming. Even so, she found herself trying to reason with him. "Now, Shane, there's no reason to overreact—"

It was too late. Even as she jumped back, he made a slashing motion reminiscent of Zorro that left a zigzagging blue trail from her armpit to her waist to the opposite hip, then stepped back to study his handiwork. "Hmm. I guess you're right."

Jessy stared at him, half amused and half in shock. The old Shane was back, all right. She could see it in the curve of his mouth, the tone of his voice, the light dancing in those dark gray eyes.

"Although," he went on thoughtfully, "it's kind of hard to tell without seeing it on your face."

"No!" She pulled back just as his hand snaked out and the roller grazed her chin. Ducking to one side, she made a grab for it as he tried again.

Clearly amused, he swung the roller out of reach and caught her seeking hand by the wrist. "What's the matter? Can't take what you dish out?"

"I most certainly—oops!" Already off balance, she slipped as she encountered a patch of paint on the plastic tarp. Certain she was going to crash to the floor, she made a desperate grab for Shane and instinctively shut her eyes, only to open them wide as she heard the roller hit the floor a second before she felt Shane's arms come around her.

"Easy." He tugged her close to steady her; she automatically brought her hands up to his shoulders to brace herself. "You all right?"

"Y-yes." Despite the paint and their clothing, she could feel every inch of him pressed against her, from the warm slab of his chest to the solid pressure of his hips and thighs. Her breath caught; she dampened her suddenly dry lips and his body shifted against hers, growing subtly harder.

She looked up and their gazes meshed.

Jessy didn't know what he saw in her face, but it caused the laughter to drain from his eyes, replaced by something dark and watchful and intense. "Shane…" Her voice trailed off when she realized she didn't know what to say.

"Damn it, Jess." His voice was a harsh whisper as he slid his hand up to her nape, tipped his head and found her mouth with his own.

Boy, did he know how to kiss. Stunned by the depth of her pleasure, Jessy tried to take it all in. The heat of his palm as he cupped her head. The welcome pressure of his fingers against the small of her back. The hard smoothness of his lips as they slanted against hers.

A tremor shook her. She'd dreamed about this so often. Yet the reality was a thousand times better than any fantasy. Her imagination hadn't done justice to how it felt to have the cool slippery silk of Shane's hair sliding between her fingers, the slight sandpaper rasp of his beard against her cheek, the solid pressure of his chest against her tender nipples.

He made an inarticulate murmur, and pulled her closer, his hands kneading her hips provocatively. Enthralled, she raked her teeth against his bottom lip. He deepened the kiss, his tongue finding the seam of her lips at the same time that his hands found the open sides of her coveralls. Without a second's hesitation, he slid his fingers, which felt cool against her fevered flesh, underneath the elastic band on her panties and cupped her bare bottom, urging her closer.

Need rushed through her. She pressed against him, gasping for breath. She tried to say the word "yes." It came out as a whimper.

To her distress, her soft cry seemed to cut right through him. All of a sudden, he went very still, his body tensed—and he abruptly snatched his hands from her shorts and tore his mouth from hers. The next thing she knew he was pushing her away.

"Shane?" She stared at him in question, dazed and more than a little shaken.

Despite the flecks of blue that dotted his face, and which she imagined must now dot hers as well, there was nothing amusing about his appearance. He was breathing hard. His gray eyes were so dark they appeared almost black, and the beautiful line of his mouth was severe. He took a hard look at her, and she winced as she had a sudden vision of herself in her old clothes, covered in paint, with strands of hair falling out of her ponytail.

"Damn it," he muttered. Abruptly he turned away, raking a hand through his hair as he struggled to get himself under control.

Perplexed by his agitation, she reached out and laid her hand on his shoulder, her whole body tight with longing. "Shane, it's all right—"

"No. It isn't." He shrugged off her hand and turned

to face her, his expression remote and unreadable. "I'm sorry," he said stiffly. "I shouldn't have done that."

Jessy blinked. "What?"

"It wasn't you," he said quickly. "I just—" he raked a hand through his hair again, revealing his agitation "—I don't know what came over me. You were just here and I lost my head. It won't happen again."

"Oh." She couldn't have felt more shattered if he'd slapped her in the face. The only blessing was that she'd soared so high and fallen so hard in such a short time that her emotions seemed to have overloaded. For the moment, at least, she felt numb.

"I'm sorry," he repeated.

"Don't worry about it." Numb or not, she had to get away before she did something stupid. Like blurt out that *she* wasn't sorry at all—that she had, in fact, relished every moment and would have liked more. A lot more. She took a step back, and then another, moving toward the door. "I think, if you wouldn't mind finishing up, I'll go. I really should get cleaned up. I...I have an appointment...to look at a condo. That is, if you're willing to stay with Chloe?"

"Yes, but—"

"Good. Oh! I bet you're worried about the carpet. Well, don't be." She toed off her old pull-on tennies, reached down and snatched them up. She knew she was babbling, but it was infinitely preferable to letting him talk. "See? Everything's fine."

"Jessy—"

"I'll see you later." She somehow dredged up a smile.

Just as she had the day before, she fled.

Only this time, she felt a thousand times worse.

* * *

Shane's controlled facade disintegrated seconds after Jessy cleared the doorway.

He swore savagely under his breath. Damn it all anyway! What the hell had possessed him to kiss her that way? How could he have done something so stupid? What had he been thinking?

He snorted in self-disgust. The answer to the last question was easy. He hadn't been *thinking* at all—at least, not with his head. Instead, for the first time in a year, he'd completely dropped the guard on his emotions and really let himself feel. Annoyance, at first, when he'd walked in and found Jessy painting without him. Then an urge to needle her, followed by dark, unexpected amusement when she'd had the nerve to paint him. And then, *bam!* Out of nowhere—lust.

Sharp. Urgent. Mindless.

For Jessy of all people. His little buddy.

Shane shook his head. Hell, if not for the lingering taste of her on his lips and the achingly clear memory of how warm and firm and sleek she'd felt beneath his hands, he wasn't sure he'd believe it himself.

But he could still taste her. And he did remember. And he sure wasn't likely to forget the urge he'd had while kissing her to give full rein to his hunger. He'd felt hard and hot. Ready. If she hadn't made that soft little sound, there was no telling what he would have done next.

But she had made that sound.

He thought about it now, trying to decide why it had gotten to him the way it had. Because, in retrospect, he realized she hadn't sounded disgusted. Or frightened or angry or even offended.

That's right. Because what she was, was shocked—

shocked at having a guy she's always considered her friend leave his handprints all over her butt.

He clenched his jaw, replaying her careful retreat, thinking about her jittery manner and the carefully polite look on her face. Oh, yeah. He'd shocked her, all right. It would serve him right if she decided to leave.

Except…he didn't want her to leave.

The realization shocked him. Yet the instant he stopped to think about it, he realized it wasn't really such a surprise.

Sometime in the past couple of weeks he'd gone from resentment to resignation to acceptance. Not for himself, he thought hastily, although her presence definitely made his life easier. But for Chloe. There was just something about Jessy—her kindness, her sunny nature, her energy—that was already having a positive effect on the toddler. Thanks to her, the child was starting to open up like a flower under a gentle sun. And after what he'd put Chloe through this past year with his failure to behave like a loving, nurturing father, he owed it to her not to screw things up.

If he hadn't already.

He'd just have to go talk to Jessy, damn it. He'd have to reassure her she had nothing to worry about where he was concerned. He'd have to repeat that what had happened wouldn't happen again. He'd have to explain that it had just been some sort of aberration.

Because it *had* been an aberration, he told himself firmly. Sure, there had been a few times recently when he'd found himself noticing little things about her, such as how soft and smooth her skin was and how nice she always smelled, but so what?

It didn't mean anything. And he didn't want it to mean anything. As far as meaningful relationships went, he'd sworn off women for good when he'd discovered Marissa's treachery. He didn't intend to go the rest of his life without sex, the way he had the past year and a half, but he did intend to be in total control of any future affairs. He'd look for somebody who knew the score, whose only interest was in having a good time, who, like him, wanted physical release and nothing more. Needless to say, Jessy didn't fit the bill.

He gave a humorless laugh. That was putting it mildly.

Still, he supposed he did owe her some sort of explanation about what had happened. But what could he say? That after more than a year, he'd let down his guard and this was the result? That his long-missing sex drive had chosen today to stage a reappearance and she just happened to get in its way? That one minute he'd felt amused and protective and the next, when he'd looked into her upturned face and found her gazing at him all wide-eyed and soft-lipped, his brain had shut down and a much more primitive part of his body had taken over? That it had everything to do with him and nothing to do with her?

Well, yeah. It was the truth, wasn't it?

Absolutely. And the sooner he got it over with, the better they'd both feel.

That decided, Shane looked impatiently around until he located the paint roller. He picked it up, carried it over to the tray and wet it with paint. In a few quick, efficient swipes, he finished off the wall because he'd promised Jessy that he would. Then he laid the roller back on the tray, stripped off his ruined shirt, wiped the bottom of his shoes and left the room.

Under the circumstances, he didn't think it would be wise to confront Jessy without all his clothes on, so he made a quick detour to his bedroom to wash and get a clean shirt. Then he strode down the hall, stopped in front of her door and knocked. "Jess?"

For a moment there was no answer. Then her voice came, soft but clear. "What is it?"

"I need to talk to you."

There was a pause. "All right."

He waited for her to come to the door. When she didn't, he turned the handle and pushed it open in the same instant that he heard her say, "Just give me a minute—"

It was too late. He had a full view of her as she stood by the bed, a T-shirt clutched in her hand, her body bare except for a provocative ice pink bikini and a matching lace bra that titillated more than they covered.

Desire, unexpected and unwanted, slammed into Shane with the force of a runaway train. As if a veil had been ripped away, he saw her with absolute clarity. No longer was she an uncertain youngster, an awkward adolescent, the sweet but gawky little sister of his best friend. Instead she was a woman in every sense of the word, from the full curve of her breasts, to the dip of her slender waist to the length of her Vegas showgirl legs.

Shane's world seemed to tilt. He suddenly wondered who the hell he thought he'd been kidding.

His libido hadn't sprung back to life for no reason.

It was her. *Jessy.* God help him, but he wanted her. A want that threatened his control when he raised his gaze to her face and got a second shock: she wanted him, too. It was evident in her parted lips, her flushed cheeks, the breathless sound of her voice as she said his name.

"Shane?"

Her tone and the slumberous look in her sky blue eyes was more than he could resist. He wanted to close the distance between them, carry her down to the bed and bury himself inside her.

He took a step forward, and then another—only to hesitate for the barest instant as a distant murmur plucked at his attention. Perplexed, he listened, until slowly it dawned on him that it was Chloe, talking to herself after awakening from her nap in the spare room.

The abrupt reminder of his daughter was like a splash of cold water. He froze. As though emerging from a fog, he suddenly wondered what the hell he was doing. He didn't want this…remember? For all the reasons he'd gone over earlier. And for one that eclipsed all the others. No matter how much he'd like to deny it, he cared about Jessy Ross. Enough to know that no matter what she might think she wanted, she deserved a hell of a lot better than him.

He took a firm hold on his emotions and forced himself to meet her gaze. "Sorry," he said harshly, taking a step back. "I didn't realize you weren't dressed."

"But—"

"We can talk later."

And with that he stepped out into the hall, shut the door on temptation and walked away.

Six

"**W**hee," Chloe exclaimed as she swung slowly through the bright summer air. "Higher, Jeddy!"

With a slight smile, Jessy complied and gave the safety seat on the swing a gentle push.

"Higher!" the little girl repeated on her backward arc.

Jessy shook her head, thinking that kids were all alike; if Chloe had her way, she'd be soaring at treetop level and to heck with the consequences. Thank goodness for both of them that the little scamp was safely strapped in—and was easily satisfied.

"Hang on," she instructed solemnly, giving the toddler only the lightest shove.

Chloe's response was a crow of delight.

The happy sound blended well with the excited shouts coming from the older kids across the way at Churchill's municipal pool, as well as the grunts and exclamations from the various groups of skateboarders and tennis players also enjoying the city's downtown park.

Across the way, sharing the sunny playground with them, were a trio of giggling preschoolers in the sandbox and a pair of gossiping grade-school kids riding a teeter-totter.

Coming here had been a good idea, Jessy decided. Thanks to an incoming tooth, Chloe had been cross and out of sorts the past few days. A change in scenery was clearly just what she'd needed.

Jessy only wished her own spirits could be improved so easily. But it would take more than a little time in a sandbox or a session on a swing to make her feel better, she thought tartly. As much as she might wish otherwise, she couldn't get what had happened the previous Sunday between her and Shane out of her mind.

Being rejected that first time, after their clinch, had hurt. So had Shane's subsequent claim that she wasn't even responsible for firing his passions. Her one consolation had been the knowledge that he hadn't cottoned on to her attraction to him. While it hadn't been much, it had provided some small comfort to her wounded pride.

Unfortunately her feeling of comfort had proved to be short-lived. She'd been feeling too raw, and her surprise had been too complete, for her to put on an act when Shane had unexpectedly caught her in her underwear. Once past her initial shock at the situation, she'd simply reacted, dropping her guard because she'd foolishly thought maybe he'd had a change of heart.

And what had it gotten her? A second rejection.

Jessy's mouth tightened. There was no use denying that Shane's abrupt retreat had cut to the quick. It was one thing for him to call a halt to things out of a misguided attempt to protect her. It was quite another for him to turn his back and walk away when he had to have seen that she didn't want to be protected. She'd felt hurt, embarrassed, humiliated.

Not surprisingly, once released from her paralysis by the sight of the door swinging shut, she'd pulled on some clothes and bolted. Yet once she'd calmed down enough to really think about what had happened, she'd realized something amazing—while Shane *had* walked away, it wasn't because he hadn't wanted her.

She might not have tons of experience, but she knew enough to know desire when she saw it.

The realization had taken the teeth out of her hurt and anger. More importantly, it had made her wonder.

About a lot of things.

For starters, why was he so intent on denying his feelings?

A few weeks ago, her answer would have been automatic: He was still mourning Marissa. Even now, it made a certain amount of sense, given that he never spoke of his late wife and there were absolutely no pictures or personal reminders of her in the house. Jessy knew, from what her own father had gone through, that there were some hurts so deep that the only way to cope was to deny their very existence.

Yet all she had to do was consider the past to decide it didn't ring true.

Although she didn't know much about Shane and Marissa's marriage—she hadn't wanted to know, at first because it was painful, and then later because it was none of her business—she was aware, through Bailey, that the relationship had had its share of problems. Yet she also knew that Shane had been elated when he'd learned he was going to be a father. And that he'd been a hands-on dad right from the start, changing diapers without a murmur, volunteering for middle-of-the-night feedings, taking time off from his business to be with his wife and daughter. And that at the time of Chloe's christening, he had appeared to be happy.

The car accident that had taken Marissa's life had changed that, of course. Shane had been devastated. Yet once the initial shock had worn off and he'd emerged from the first overwhelming wave of grief, he'd seemed to be making a tremendous effort to pull himself together. He'd told Bailey at the time that he felt he had to be strong for Chloe's sake. Yet Jessy could remember thinking that his courage and resolve stemmed as much from the force of his own character as his need to be there for his daughter; Shane had always been centered, with a basic belief in the goodness of life. While Jessy had mourned for his loss, she'd never doubted he would be all right. He was a survivor.

Perhaps that was why she'd been so taken aback by the changes she'd seen in him at Chloe's first birthday party. It had been six months since the accident. She'd expected there would be moments of sadness that day, just as she'd been prepared for Shane to be quieter and more somber than usual. After all, the party at his parents' house had been the first full gathering of his family and close friends since the funeral.

What she hadn't anticipated was that he would be so…detached. Gone was the warmth, the spontaneity, the approachability that had always been so much a part of him. Instead he'd had the air of a man operating under some great restraint, and though at first Jessy had assumed he was just trying to contain his grief, as the party had worn on she'd had the uncomfortable thought that he was playing a role: Recently Widowed Father Bearing Up Well. Beneath that faultless facade, however, he'd seemed remote, withdrawn, almost angry.

It had been a disturbing insight, one she'd struggled against, telling herself that she was mistaken or that it was simply one of the stages of grief, and that he'd get over it.

But he hadn't.

Still, if he wasn't mourning Marissa, then…what?

Jessy shook her head, not certain of any of the answers. And even if she was, she realized, it wouldn't solve her more immediate problem: For the past four days, Shane had once again taken to avoiding her.

She sighed. In all fairness, she had to admit that he wasn't solely to blame, at least not initially. She'd been the one who'd stayed away the first night, not coming home until late because she hadn't quite known how to face him. And she had to admit that she'd been relieved when she'd found him already gone when she got up the next morning.

Yet it hadn't taken her long to realize how foolishly she was behaving. Thanks to her parents' example, she knew very well that nothing ever got solved by brushing it under the rug. It was always better to get the issue out in the open, face it head-on and try to resolve it.

Which was exactly what she was prepared to do—if Shane would only cooperate. Unfortunately they seemed to be back where they'd started, with him going to work early and coming home late. And though Jessy might have been willing to be patient under different circumstances, might even have been willing to wait for him to realize that withdrawing wasn't going to accomplish anything, she had Chloe to consider.

Instead of getting to spend more time with her father—which was, Jessy was quick to remind herself, why she'd offered to move in with Shane in the first place—the toddler was once again seeing him less.

So? What are you going to do about it?

More to the point, what *could* she do about it?

Her expression thoughtful, she gave Chloe another little push and began to consider her options.

Shane glanced up as his office door opened. Still holding the sales report he'd been studying, he looked over inquiringly at the temp who was filling in for Grace, his secretary. "What is it, Jeffrey?"

The younger man took a step forward as if to approach the desk, then appeared to think better of it. "There's somebody here to see you."

He frowned, then deliberately returned his attention to the papers in his hand, wondering irritably why the hell the temp hadn't simply buzzed him on the intercom. "Does this person have an appointment?"

"No, but—"

"Is it an emergency?"

"Well no, sir, I don't believe so, but—"

"I believe I told you I didn't want to be interrupted."

"Yes, you did, but I thought—it's your baby-sitter, Miss Ross."

Shane's head snapped up. "What?"

"She's out in the reception area with your daughter—"

"Actually she's not."

Jessy's familiar, slightly husky voice drew Shane's gaze to where she stood framed in the doorway, Chloe propped on her hip.

"Dada," the toddler chirped happily.

He managed a tight smile and climbed to his feet. "Hey, Chloe." He shifted his gaze to Jessy. To his disgust, he immediately found himself wondering what sort of lace temptation she had on under her deceptively casual black shorts and pale green T-shirt. "Hi," he said a little stiffly.

"Hi," she responded, stepping past Jeffrey and into the room. "I hope I'm not interrupting. Chloe and I were at the park, and I thought as long as we were so close, I'd take a chance and see if you were in. I'd like to talk to you if you have a minute."

He hesitated, briefly tempted to tell her he was on his way out. After a moment of reflection, however, his common sense asserted itself. He supposed they might as well get this—whatever "this" was—over with. He inclined his head. "Sure."

"Good." Responding to Chloe's squirming, she leaned over and set the child on the ground.

"I 'winged," the little girl said, heading straight for him.

"That's great," he said absently, his focus on Jessy.

"I goed *waaay* up," she informed him, tugging on his sleeve.

He glanced down at her earnest little face, then back at Jessy, who was looking around at the navy leather couch, the big executive desk, the computer station that wrapped one corner.

"I goed high, high, high," Chloe persisted, raising her arms to him.

With an inner sigh, Shane reluctantly shifted his attention to the child. "You did, huh?" She nodded emphatically, and something inside him softened. He reached down and lifted her up. "I guess that means you had fun at the park, then."

She nodded again, then hooked an arm around his neck and began to play with his tie.

He caught a slight movement out of the corner of his eye and realized that his secretary was still standing in the doorway. He looked over, inexplicably irritated as he saw the admiring way the young man was staring at Jessy's backside. "That'll be all, Mr. Bradley," he said coolly.

The temp gave a guilty start. His gaze met Shane's, then he looked hastily away and took an abrupt step back. "Oh, yeah. Right." He quickly shut the door.

"He's very nice," Jessy said mildly.

"Yeah. I guess." Shane hadn't given it much thought one way or the other.

She walked over to study the gallery of framed photos that covered one wall, bending slightly when one caught her eye. "It's too bad his fiancée broke things off, but I guess it's her loss."

He felt his eyes narrowing. "How long were you out there, anyway?"

She shrugged. "I don't know. Not long. But we have talked several times on the phone this week."

Shane frowned. In the two weeks Jeffrey had worked for him, he'd found the young man to be organized, efficient and unobtrusive. For the first time, however, it occurred to him that the temp wasn't exactly ugly, and that he and Jessy must be about the same age.

For some reason, the thought increased his annoyance. "Look," he said impatiently, pacing to one corner of the desk. "It's nice of you to drop by, but I'm afraid I've got work to do, so if you could just get to the point—"

"Of course." She turned to face him, her voice reassuring. "This shouldn't take long."

She was going to tell him she couldn't take care of Chloe any longer. He knew it with sudden certainty. Ei-

ther that, or she was going to say something else he
didn't want to hear, such as how much she cared about
him—

"I just want you to know it's safe to come home,"
she said lightly.

"What?"

"You don't have to stay away," she said, rephrasing.
"I swear I won't attack you or anything." A faint, self-
deprecating smile warmed her face. "I promise."

"Jessy—"

She raised her hand to silence him, which was a damn
good thing since he didn't have a clue what he was going
to say.

"I'm willing to forget what happened if you are," she
went on in the same reasonable, good-natured voice.
"We can just write it off as a temporary moment of
madness. I mean, I'd be lying if I didn't admit that kissing you fulfilled an old adolescent fantasy of mine. Or
that for a little while there, I sort of regressed back to
my teen years and lost my head. But I can see now that
it was no big deal. After all, we're both adults, and one
insignificant little kiss and a few seconds of you seeing
me in my underwear shouldn't matter. Right?"

"Right." Shane nodded, telling himself he was in total agreement. And that instead of this continuing irritation, what he ought to feel was relieved. She wasn't
leaving. That was the important thing.

Yet he had to admit it rankled to have her reduce what
had happened between them to the status of old adolescent fantasy. And he sure as hell wouldn't call the kiss
they'd shared either little or insignificant.

Not that he cared or anything. What mattered was that
Jessy believed it. That was what was important. Because,
despite her attempt at humor, he sure as hell hadn't

stayed away because he was afraid to be around her. He'd stayed away solely for her sake, to give her some time to think and to get her act together. If she was willing to forgive and forget, to act as if Sunday had never happened, it was fine by him. After all, nothing had changed on his end except that he'd finally quit thinking of her as if she still had scabs on her knees and started to think of her as a woman.

Yeah. An extremely desirable woman.

But then, so what? Even if he were aware of her in a way he hadn't been before, he was confident he could handle it. How hard could it be? It wasn't as if she were some "Baywatch" babe who made it a habit to stroll around the house half dressed, much less a femme fatale who was going to slip uninvited into his bed.

He'd managed to survive without sex for more than a year and a half. He sure as hell could manage a month or two longer.

Careful to keep his expression neutral, he met her gaze squarely as she walked closer and held out her hand. "So what do you say?" she said softly. "Friends?"

"Sure." He reached out, clasped her hand and gave it a businesslike, one-adult-to-another shake. He told himself to ignore how incredibly soft her skin felt. And how perfectly her hand fit within his.

He could handle this.

The intercom buzzed. Giving her a nod, he released her hand and turned toward the phone, picking up the receiver. One-handed, he stabbed the button for the secretary's desk. "What is it, Jeffrey?"

"I'm sorry to interrupt, Mr. Wyatt, but Marcus Finch is on line one."

Finch was the chief financial officer for his Dallas supplier. "Fine. Thanks. I'll get it."

He waited for the temp to hang up, then looked over at Jessy. "Sorry. I've got to take this."

Her smile was bright and sunny. "No problem. I'm supposed to take a look at a condo in a little while, anyway. We'll let you get back to work. Say goodbye to Daddy," she said to Chloe.

"Bye-bye, Dada," the child said cheerfully.

Jessy reached across him and took the child from his arms. "I'll see you for dinner, then?" She settled the toddler on her hip.

"Sure." In a demonstration of control, he ignored the tight feeling that had come over him when she'd brushed against him.

No matter what it took, he could handle this.

Shane came home at the end of the day as promised.

That was the good news, Jessy told herself, sneaking a peak at him across the dinner table.

The bad news was that while his voluntary exile might be over, the camaraderie of the preceding weekend appeared to be history. He might be here physically, but they weren't back on their prekiss footing by any stretch of the imagination.

Instead, in the two hours since he'd walked in the door, he'd been remote, contained, almost...wary. So much so that if Jessy didn't know better, she'd think he really believed that if he wasn't careful she'd sneak up, tie him to the nearest bed and have her wicked way with him.

Which was ridiculous. Shane was an intelligent man. He had to know that her reassurance of his safety had been a joke, a face-saving way to break the ice and downplay what had transpired between them.

Didn't he?

Of course he did. There was no reason for her to be sitting here now, hours later, worrying about it.

But then again... He could say *something* to indicate he realized that *he* had kissed *her* last Sunday and not the other way around, she thought, pushing a bite-size piece of chicken around her plate with her fork. After all, it wasn't as if it would kill him to try to put her at ease for a change.

She frowned, suddenly wondering what was wrong with her. Shane was home, having dinner with his daughter, just the way she'd wanted. So what was her problem?

She sighed, and reluctantly admitted that perhaps she hadn't thought things through as well as she might have before going to his office. The truth was, she'd been so busy the past few days worrying about what he felt, she hadn't devoted much thought to her own emotions. Oh, she'd reviewed what had happened between them endlessly, and she'd acknowledged that his rejection hurt, but she hadn't let herself think beyond that to how she currently felt. Particularly about Shane.

She hesitated, then told herself there was no use lying about it. Despite everything that had happened, she still felt attracted to him. Powerfully, undeniably attracted.

And she was darned if she understood it. Never in her life had her thoughts been quite so sexual. Heaven help her, but even now, when she was feeling more than a little out of sorts, she still found herself noticing things about him that she shouldn't.

Like how thick and shiny his hair was. And what broad shoulders he had. And how deft and sure his fingers were as he used his knife and fork.

Clearly if they were going to have a chance at putting

their relationship back the way it had been before, she had to get past her preoccupation with his body.

It was just...she wasn't sure how to do it. Or even if she could, she admitted, glancing over at him. Because, when you got right down to it, he really was wonderful to look at, with that straight nose, and that chiseled mouth, and those dark, heavily lashed eyes. And then there was that body—

With a start, she realized what she was doing. Disgusted with herself—she really had to get a grip—she cast about for a topic of conversation, determined to do whatever she had to for a distraction.

"So." She sat up straighter. "How did your phone call go?"

As subjects went, it wasn't exactly brilliant. But then, she wasn't exactly at her best. And she'd already brought up the weather, her and Chloe's time at the park and the postcard that had come from his mother. Short of asking him outright to put a bag on his head, it was the best that she could do.

He looked at her with a sort of guarded surprise. "It went fine."

She waited, but he didn't elaborate. "That's good."

"Uh-huh."

"I'm afraid I didn't have as much luck with the condo."

"Mmm."

She wrinkled her nose, determined not to take offense at his lack of interest, although she was once again starting to feel exasperated. "The unit was beautiful, but the complex was kind of stuffy. I'm looking for someplace more mellow. Someplace where I don't have to put on my pearls to go to the mailbox."

"I see." He laid his fork on his empty plate.

"Are you finished?"

"Yeah. Thanks."

"There's pie for dessert."

"I'll pass."

Gosh, why wasn't she surprised? On the other hand, it was probably for the best, since she'd definitely had enough—of everything. She laid down her own fork. The quicker they put an end to this meal, the better.

Climbing to her feet, she began to gather their dishes to carry them into the kitchen, only to stop as she glanced over at Chloe and saw the toddler had her hands stuck in her applesauce and was thoughtfully squishing it through her fingers.

After eating three meals a day with the child for close to a month, Jessy was pretty sure she knew what was coming. "Chloe no—!" she began.

She was too late. She'd no more than said the first syllable of the child's name when the toddler leaned over and dropped her face in the bowl.

Under different circumstances, Jessy probably would have thought it was funny. At the moment, however, it just seemed to be one more example of how nothing was going the way it should. Pursing her lips, she ignored the applesauce slowly oozing over the side of the bowl and waited for Chloe to surface.

It didn't take long. Not more than a few seconds passed before the child gingerly raised her head. She stared at Jessy uncertainly, taking in her disapproving expression. "Uh-oh," she said in a tiny voice.

"Uh-oh is right," Jessy replied sternly, not wanting the little girl to start thinking what she'd done was acceptable. Even if it was sort of cute, in an extremely messy way. "That was a big no-no, young lady."

Chloe's bottom lip quivered pathetically.

Jessy suddenly felt like the Wicked Witch of the West. Apparently she wasn't the only one to think so, either, if the faint sound of protest she heard issue from the far side of the table was any indication.

She glanced over to find Mr. I-Don't-Have-Anything-To-Say sitting there with a frown on his face that said clearly he thought she was being too hard on his child.

It was the last straw. She felt a flash of annoyance. Fast on its heels came a sudden calm, however, as she abruptly realized that Shane was right. She was out of line. After all, there was no reason to get mad at Chloe when *he* was the one who was ticking her off.

"However—" she turned back to the child "—I guess it's okay this time since I know how much Daddy is going to enjoy getting you cleaned up and ready for bed."

"What?" There was a scraping sound as Shane's chair slid back.

"You don't mind, do you?" Keeping her expression as bland as her voice, she carried the load of dirty dishes into the kitchen. "After all, I've already bathed her once today, when we got back from town. And I've still got these dishes to do and a load of laundry to fold—"

"All right already," he said abruptly. "I'll take care of it."

"Good." She set down the dishes and dampened a paper towel, which she handed to him when she walked back over to finish clearing the table.

He glanced from the paper towel to her, and then at Chloe, who stared cheerfully back at him as applesauce dripped from her hair onto her face. "Dada," she cooed, already perking up. "Goody."

Shane plucked the paper towel from Jessy's grasp. "Thanks a lot."

"You're welcome." Struggling to keep a straight face, she began to clear the table, watching out of the corner of her eye as he carefully wiped Chloe off, lifted her from the high chair and carried her out of the room at arms length, presumably headed for the bathroom.

The second he disappeared from sight, the grin she'd been fighting took over.

No doubt about it. She was definitely feeling better.

Okay, so maybe that's the answer to your attraction to Shane. Just keep it light and easy—and don't spend too much time in the same room with him—and you'll be okay.

Maybe. Yet somehow Jessy doubted that it was really going to be that easy.

Seven

The house was quiet when Shane got home from the office Friday afternoon.

Closing the door from the garage behind him, he walked across the utility room and paused on the threshold to the kitchen. It and the family room were deserted.

For a moment he felt strangely let down. Then he shrugged it off, making a conscious decision not to be stupid. What did he expect? That Chloe and Jess would be standing at the door, waiting for him with bated breath?

He told himself to get real as he crossed the lengthening fingers of sunshine that slanted across the floor. Such an ambition would have been silly under any circumstances. But given the current air of restraint between him and Jessy, not to mention that he was home early and she wasn't expecting him, it was really foolish.

Besides, it wasn't as if he couldn't use a little time to

unwind, he reflected, as he tossed his suit coat over the back of a stool and loosened his tie. The past few days at work had been intense. He was looking forward to the weekend. A nice, quiet, *uneventful* weekend.

Not that he expected anything else, he thought as he sorted through the mail. The past few days had gone just the way he intended. Sure, there had been some awkward moments. One had occurred last night at dinner when he and Jess had simultaneously reached for the margarine at the dinner table and their hands touched. And he'd been literally knocked off balance this morning when she'd walked sleepily out of her bedroom and right into his arms as he'd been leaving for work.

Yet neither incident had amounted to much. A swift move away, a polite nod and a murmur of apology had taken care of both. He had everything well under control.

He was halfway down the hall, headed for his bedroom, when he heard the music. Cocking his head, he realized what he was hearing was a radio as the tune faded and an announcer came on, his voice a suave murmur. Seconds later, a new song started, this one a powerful, catchy love song.

Shane stopped at the door to Chloe's room.

Just like last Sunday, Jessy was at work inside. Only today she wasn't painting. Instead she was standing on a step stool. She had her back to him and she was applying a wallpaper border.

He watched as she reached up, leaned slightly to her left and painstakingly began to smooth a section of the brightly colored paper into place, balancing the rest of the strip, which was folded into a sort of loose bundle, on her shoulder.

She was barefoot, he noted. And—he couldn't refrain

from a frown—she was dressed in a fire engine red crop top and an abbreviated pair of cutoffs.

She was also singing enthusiastically along with the song. After a moment, her hips picked up the strong, slow beat, causing several long pieces of fringe trailing from her cutoffs to swish tantalizingly back and forth against her thighs.

Damn, but the air felt stuffy all of a sudden. He couldn't seem to breathe properly. He tried to tell himself the problem was lingering paint fumes.

And he might have even believed it except he couldn't seem to drag his gaze away from Jessy's backside. Or stop himself from wondering what it would be like to move up behind her and replace that fringe with his hands.

Somehow he knew that her skin would feel like sun-warmed satin, while her buttocks would be cool and firm, just the right size to fill his palms....

He shifted restlessly. He felt strange, his skin hot and tight, as if it were a size too small for his body.

Oblivious to his presence, Jessy dropped back on her heels. She shifted the rolled strip off her shoulder and had just begun to unwind another section of border when she finally caught sight of him out of the corner of her eye.

"Shane!" Clearly startled, she pivoted around. For a second she seemed on the verge of losing her temper, but if so she quickly got control of herself. "What is it with you?" she inquired reasonably enough. "Do you enjoy sneaking up on people?"

Seen from the front, the crop top exposed way too much of her smooth, golden stomach. There was no way he could miss seeing the shadowed indentation of her navel. Or how her waist nipped in above her hips.

That tight feeling grew worse. "Sorry." With an act of will, he dragged his gaze from her midriff to her face. "If you hadn't been so caught up in your Barbra Streisand routine, you would have heard me come in."

"You heard that?"

"'Fraid so."

She hesitated a second, then caught him totally unprepared when she grinned. "Well, I guess that'll teach you to tiptoe around."

To his acute surprise, he felt an answering flash of amusement. Grateful for the distraction, he managed a faint smile of his own. "Yeah. I guess. Although, it does seem like cruel and unusual punishment."

She narrowed her eyes in mock disgust. "Very funny, Wyatt."

For a moment it was like old times, when their relationship had been warm and uncomplicated.

Yet as their gazes continued to meet, Shane felt the welcome protection of his amusement fade. In its place was something hot and elemental.

He tried to deny it. Just as he tried to deny the urge he suddenly had to close the distance between them, rub his cheek against the satiny sleekness of Jessy's abdomen, dip his tongue into her shallow navel, slide his hands under that flimsy little top—

"Gosh!" Jessy exclaimed brightly, tearing her gaze from his. "I wonder why Chloe isn't up from her nap? What time is it, anyway? Did you hear her when you came in?"

Her innocent flood of questions jerked him back to reality. Pressing his shoulder to the doorjamb, he thrust his hands in his front pockets so keep himself from doing something irretrievably stupid. Damn it. What the hell was wrong with him?

He took a firm rein on his runaway hormones and tried to remember what she'd just said. "Relax," he said finally as it came back to him. He twisted his wrist far enough to see his watch. "It's just after four. I'm home early. She's probably still asleep."

"Oh." She flashed him a relieved smile. "In that case, I suppose I'd better quit talking and start working before she does wake up."

"Yeah. I think I'll go for a run."

"Good idea," she said heartily. "I'll see you later then." Without further ado, she turned around and began to unroll another section of wallpaper, humming along as an Elton John song came on the radio.

Well, hell. She didn't have to sound so cheerful about it.

Aware he was behaving irrationally, but thoroughly out of sorts anyway, he continued to watch her—until he found his gaze skating down the shapely length of her legs.

He averted his eyes with a jerk, turned on his heel and hightailed it toward his room, his thoughts churning.

What the hell was he trying to do? Make himself crazy? Tempt fate?

No. No to all of those things. He was just tired. And dealing with a lot of work-related stress. He'd go for a few laps around the lake—all right, make that a few laps *in* the lake—and in no time at all he'd have his head screwed on straight.

No problem. Really. He could handle this.

Jessy stood in the hall outside the bathroom, listening to the low rumble of Shane's voice as he responded to Chloe's happy chatter.

So far, so good, she told herself, shifting her hold on

the stack of towels in her arms. Her strategy of acting cheerful and upbeat around Shane seemed to be paying off. Although he still seemed rather tense, he *had* come home early today, and after dinner tonight he had even volunteered to give Chloe a bath.

She had nobody but herself to blame that the past twenty-four hours had been harder than she could have imagined. Or that no matter how hard she tried, she couldn't convince herself that what she felt for Shane was mere friendly affection. Or that because she'd never been very good at pretense, the strain of her constant cheeriness was already starting to tell.

She shook her head, thinking about her encounter earlier in Chloe's room with Shane. She'd nearly blown it when she'd turned around and found him standing in the doorway, looking hopelessly appealing with his tie loosened and his shirt unbuttoned. She'd been so flustered and off balance that for a few seconds there, she'd imagined she saw a flicker of desire shining in the silvery gray of his eyes.

But no. As his perfectly pleasant responses had quickly shown, she'd been indulging in wishful thinking. Just because she'd felt a certain way was no reason to project those feelings onto him. Particularly when he seemed oblivious to her inner struggle—and she very much wanted to keep it that way.

That was why, in addition to being bright and sunny, she'd decided it wouldn't hurt to give him—and herself—some space the next two days. The only reason she was here now, about to intrude on Chloe's bath time, was because she'd washed towels today and hadn't had time yet to put them away. She didn't intend to linger. She'd be in and out in no time.

She took a deep breath, plastered a smile on her face and walked across the threshold. "Hi. How's it going?"

Shane looked up from where he was kneeling beside the tub. For a second she could have sworn there was a flash of something dark and dangerous in his eyes as he looked at her, but then his lashes came down, veiling his expression. "Fine."

"Lookee, Jeddy!" Scooting forward, Chloe flopped tummy down in the shallow water and began to energetically thrash her arms and legs. "I 'wimming!"

Jessy smiled despite herself. "That's very good, sweetie."

"That's also enough," Shane said hastily, raising a hand to shield his eyes as water sprayed all over him. "I already told you, no swimming in the tub."

"Daddy's right," she said as the toddler glanced questioningly at her. To Shane, she added dryly, "I thought you might need some towels." She walked over and set the stack on the counter. After a glance at the water dotting him and the floor, she peeled one off the pile and handed it to him.

He rubbed it over his hair and face, then started in on the floor. "Thanks."

"You're welcome." She watched the material of his shirt strain across his shoulders. If he wasn't careful, he was going to pop his buttons. Or split the denim of those ancient jeans, which were already white where they stretched across his firm buttocks—

Jessy swallowed. It was definitely time to make an exit. "Well." Her voice sounded husky to her own ears. "I'll leave you to it." She edged toward the door, which seemed terribly far away given how small the bathroom suddenly felt.

"No! Jeddy stay," Chloe said instantly, scrambling into a sitting position. "Do bubbas," she demanded.

"Chloe—"

"Pwease?"

Jessy looked down at her in consternation. The toddler had requested "bubbas" before. Then and now, Jessy would have been happy to comply—if only she knew what the toddler was talking about. Unfortunately she didn't have a clue.

Salvation came from an unexpected source. "Jessy doesn't want to get all wet tonight, Chlo," Shane said firmly. "Daddy will do it, okay?"

"Okay!" the toddler exclaimed happily.

Jessy stared at the back of his well-shaped head. "You will?"

"Sure."

"Oh." Every instinct she possessed told her she should leave—now—before she said or did something stupid. Yet how could she when the mystery of bubbas was about to be revealed? "Do you need some help?"

"Nope. Although you could hand me the shampoo."

"No problem." She got it from the childproof cupboard, then grabbed a towel and tossed it to the floor, using the folded cotton to cushion her knees as she sank down beside him.

Shane looked at her, his gaze hooded as he plucked the shampoo from her hand. "I can handle this. Really."

"Of course you can," she said quickly, her fingers tingling from the brush of his. "I just thought I'd stick around and check out your...technique." She winced. *Great choice of words, Jess.*

He shrugged. "Suit yourself." He poured a dollop of shampoo in his palm, his shoulder bumping hers as he leaned over and worked the amber liquid through

Chloe's pale, fine hair. Once he had a dense lather, he deftly began to sculpt the child's hair into a series of spikes that stuck out all over her head. "There." He rinsed his hands in the water and dried them with the towel.

Jessy stared at Chloe's soap-covered head. "That's it?"

"Yeah." He paused, then asked almost reluctantly, "What did you expect?"

"Oh, nothing," she said hastily. "I—it's perfect."

He looked over at her. "I do know how to do a few things, you know."

Jessy glanced back at him, and the instant their eyes met she knew she'd made a mistake. He was so close she could see the tiny flecks of silver and black in his eyes. More alarming, she wanted to kiss away the tension she could see tightening the corners of his mouth. It would be easy, really. All she would have to do was lean forward, turn her head slightly to the side, then gently press her lips to his—

"Dada?" Chloe interrupted. "See bubbas?"

A slight shudder seemed to go through Shane. He tore his gaze away, focusing his attention on his daughter. "Yeah. Of course." Twisting around, he snagged the hand mirror off the counter, his thigh pressing against Jessy's in the process. He held up the mirror so Chloe could see herself.

"Oooh!" The toddler reached out and wrapped her little hand around his to bring the mirror closer, then reached up and moved a spike in a different direction. Her eyes lit up. "Pretty, pretty bubbas," she proclaimed, turning her head this way and that as she admired her punklike hairstyle.

His glance strayed briefly back to Jessy, flicked from

her eyes to her mouth, then abruptly shifted back to Chloe. "Yeah," he murmured. "Pretty."

Jessy sat rooted to the spot. She knew it was foolish, but for a second there, it was almost as if he'd actually been referring to her.

Which just went to show why it was a bad idea for her to spend too much time around him. Ten minutes in close proximity, and she was imagining all sorts of unlikely things.

It was obviously time for her to leave.

"Well." She rocked back on her heels and came to her feet. "I can see that you have everything under control. And since I have the rest of the laundry to put away, I'll see you two when you're all done, okay?"

Shane nodded, looking as cool and composed as ever. "Okay." It wasn't until she was almost to the door that he added, "Hey, Jess?"

In the split second it took her to answer, her imagination went wild. Maybe he'd tell her he was looking forward to "later." Or maybe he'd ask her not to go. "What?"

"Thanks for the towels."

Heat rose in her cheeks. She really had to get a grip on herself! "You're welcome," she murmured.

She bolted.

Shane lay in bed, idly contemplating the play of morning sunshine across the ceiling. He'd been awake for a good half hour; he supposed he ought to get up.

On the other hand, what was the rush? It was nice to lounge in bed for a change. And, since he'd heard Jessy with Chloe out in the hall earlier, there was no reason he couldn't stay right where he was.

Yeah, maybe you can stay in bed all day. Better yet,

PLAY

RUN
FOR THE
ROSES

and get

THREE FREE GIFTS!

HOW TO PLAY:

1. With a coin, carefully scratch off the silver box at the right. Then check the claim chart to see what we have for you — **FREE BOOKS** and a **FREE GIFT** — **ALL YOURS FREE**

2. Send back the card and you'll receive two brand-new Silhouette Desire® novels. These books have a cover price of $3.75 each, but they are yours to keep absolutely free

3. There's no catch. You're under no obligation to buy anything. We charge nothing — ZERO — for your first shipment. And you don't have to make any minimum number of purchases — not even one!

4. The fact is, thousands of readers enjoy receiving books by mail from the Silhouette Reader Service™. They like the convenience of home delivery...they like getting the best new novels months before they're available in stores...and they love our discount prices

5. We hope that after receiving your free books you'll want to remain a subscriber. But the choice is yours — to continue or cancel, any time at all! So why not take us up on our invitation, with no risk of any kind. You'll be glad you did!

This surprise mystery gift
Will be yours **FREE** –
When you play
RUN for the ROSES

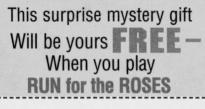

The Silhouette Reader Service™ — Here's how it works:

Accepting free books places you under no obligation to buy anything. You may keep the books and gift and return the shipping statement marked "cancel." If you do not cancel, about a month later we'll send you 6 additional novels and bill you just $3.12 each, plus 25¢ delivery per book and applicable sales tax, if any.* That's the complete price — and compared to cover prices of $3.75 each — quite a bargain! You may cancel at any time, but if you choose to continue, every month we'll send you 6 more books, which you may either purchase at the discount price...or return to us and cancel your subscription.

*Terms and prices subject to change without notice. Sales tax applicable in N.Y.

If offer card is missing write to: Silhouette Reader Service, 3010 Walden Ave., P.O. Box 1867, Buffalo NY 14240-1867

BUSINESS REPLY MAIL
FIRST-CLASS MAIL   PERMIT NO. 717   BUFFALO, NY

POSTAGE WILL BE PAID BY ADDRESSEE

SILHOUETTE READER SERVICE
3010 WALDEN AVE
PO BOX 1867
BUFFALO NY 14240-9952

NO POSTAGE
NECESSARY
IF MAILED
IN THE
UNITED STATES

maybe you should lock the door and stay here for the rest of the weekend. That way you could avoid Jessy entirely.

He scowled. Not for the first time, he wondered what it would take to permanently shut off that irritating inner voice. And why the damn thing always seemed to be right on target when it came to pointing out things he'd rather avoid.

Like Jessy.

His scowl deepened. All right. So maybe ignoring her—or, more precisely, ignoring his response to her— was turning out to be far more difficult than he'd imagined. It didn't mean anything—except that once turned on, certain basic drives could be pretty damned powerful. He could handle it.

Right. You've done such a great job of it so far. Damn, man, you practically drooled while she was hanging the wallpaper. And what was that stuff in the bathroom? First you give her the cold shoulder, next you engage in a staring match with her and then you make that remark about "pretty."

Okay. He was willing to concede that he hadn't conducted himself as well as he might have. But then again, two brief slips didn't mean much. He'd been tired. Worn down from a busy week. More to the point, it had been so long since he'd had to put a leash on his libido, he was out of practice.

And it wasn't as if Jessy had helped things. Sure, she'd changed from that body baring crop top and cutoffs she'd wallpapered in into a T-shirt and short-alls for dinner, but it wasn't as if she'd done him a big favor. While the new outfit had been demure from the back and front, he'd had a perfect view from the side of the alluring way her T-shirt clung to her breasts and torso.

It had been enough to put his teeth on edge all through the meal.

Of course, that wasn't the worst of it. The worst of it was that no matter what he said or how he acted, she remained nice.

Today, however, was a new day. No matter what it took, he was going to be on top of things. After all, he was a civilized adult, not some hormone-driven teenager.

Yawning, he climbed out of bed and made a quick trip to the bathroom. He contemplated taking a shower, then decided to throw on some clothes and go get a cup of coffee first. Finger-combing his hair, he headed for the kitchen.

Chloe, who was seated in her high chair, smiled happily when she saw him, revealing a mouth filled with banana and toast. "Dada!"

"Hey, Chlo—" he began, only to break off as he caught sight of Jessy at the far end of the family room. To his alarm, she was perched atop one of the swivel stools. "What are you, nuts?" he barked, all of his good intentions to be calm and pleasant buried by an avalanche of concern. He stomped across the area rug in a few furious strides. "What the hell do you think you're doing?"

She turned to peer over her shoulder at him, nearly giving him heart failure as the chair top twisted beneath her. "Good morning." She smiled, as annoyingly cheerful as ever. "I thought I'd change this lightbulb. I noticed yesterday that it was out."

The lightbulb she was referring to just happened to be in one of the recessed cans that were set into the high, angled ceiling. He took a firm grip on his temper. "Why aren't you using the step stool?"

"I couldn't find it."

He scowled as he realized he'd used it in the garage last night. "I know where it is. Why don't you get down and I'll go get it."

"Don't bother. I don't think it would be tall enough anyway. This is fine. It's just the right height for this ceiling."

"It might be the right height, but it's dangerous. Get down and I'll go get the ladder."

"I'm fine, Shane. Really. I'm almost done."

He glared at her, wondering why she had to be so stubborn.

"Here. Take this—" she leaned over and carefully held out the used bulb "—and hand me the new one, would you?" She indicated the package sitting on an end table. Against his better judgment, he did as she asked, swearing under his breath as she straightened, stretched as far as she could and began to screw in the bulb. "There."

Thank God. It was done. "Great. Now get down before—" A jarring bang spun him around. He tensed, prepared to take action until he saw that it was nothing serious. In a fit of enterprise, Chloe had managed to pry loose the suction cup on the bottom of her plastic bowl and had dropped it—cereal and all—on the floor. Except for the mess, it was no big deal.

He started to relax, only to tighten up all over again as he heard Jessy say, "Uh-oh."

Twisting toward her, he saw that she'd turned to check things out, too. Now, the chair seat under her feet was shifting madly back and forth. He reached out to steady it, only to check his motion as Jessy gave a cry of alarm, windmilled her arms, then suddenly overbalanced. He had no time to brace as she shrieked and did a swan dive into his arms.

They slammed to the floor.

The thick rug absorbed the worst of the impact. Even so, it took Shane several minutes to get his breath back and to decide that he hadn't broken anything.

The process wasn't helped by the fact that Jessy was lying on top of him.

"Shane?"

He opened his eyes and found himself staring straight into hers, only a handful of inches away. "What?"

"Are you all right?"

Damn, but her eyes were blue. And her complexion… It was golden smooth, as finely textured as Chloe's. "Sure." He took a deep breath and the sweetness of her scent filled his head. "What about you?"

"Me? I'm fine. You broke my fall."

"Good." The word came out sounding curt, thanks to his sudden, acute awareness of her. He could feel the tickle of her hair as it brushed his neck, the warm weight of her breasts as they pressed against his chest, the silky length of her bare legs tangled with his. He shifted, trying to lessen their full frontal contact without being obvious as his body reacted.

Her eyes widened slightly, and a faint flush bloomed on her cheeks. "Oh, dear. I—I'm crushing you, aren't I?"

It was as good an excuse as any. "As a matter of fact…"

They stared at each other a second longer. Then, as if by mutual accord, they both launched into motion, Jessy rolling to one side and twisting upright into a sitting position while he scrambled in the opposite direction and did the same.

Safely separated, they regarded each other. Tucking a strand of hair behind her ear, Jessy surprised him with a rueful smile. "I guess this is where I say I'm sorry," she said lightly, absently rubbing her ankle. "I should have let you get the ladder."

"Yeah, you should have." He frowned as she continued to massage her leg. "What's the matter?"

Her hand stilled. "It's nothing. I must have knocked my ankle on something when I fell."

He hesitated, torn between concern for her and a strong awareness of the aroused state of his body. Not that there was really a question about what he was going to do. He sighed. "You'd better let me take a look."

"It's no big deal, really—"

She fell silent as he leaned forward and impatiently brushed her hands away. Wrapping one hand around her foot, he began to probe with the other, gently pressing his fingers to her flesh.

"Does that hurt?" he asked, pretending not to notice how silky soft her skin was as he carefully examined her ankle.

"No."

Gritting his teeth, he continued to probe, working his way inch by inch until he was all the way to her calf.

Jessy caught her breath.

He looked up. "What about that?"

"No."

"Then what's the matter?"

"Nothing!" she said sharply. Before he could stop her, she surprised him by pulling her leg free of his grasp and scrambling to her feet. "That's what I'm trying to tell you, if you'd just listen! I'm fine. I'm great! There's nothing wrong with me!"

He looked up at her, taken aback by her sudden vehemence and by the flush he could see in her cheeks.

"Hey, mellow out," he said, suddenly feeling more than a little tense himself. "I was only trying to help."

To his astonishment, her temper vanished. "Oh, Lord. I'm sorry. I know you were." She took a deep breath, then leaned over and offered him a hand, looking abashed. "And I appreciate it. Really."

For some reason, her friendly gesture made him feel even crankier. Ignoring her hand, he climbed to his feet. "Forget it," he said tersely. "Just forget the whole thing. I'm going to go take a shower."

"Okay." She nodded, then walked across the room, bent over and retrieved Chloe's bowl.

It didn't escape his notice that she was limping slightly, but he was damned if he was going to say anything.

She straightened. "Are you going to want breakfast when you get done?"

"No." All of a sudden he wasn't quite sure what he wanted, but he knew it wasn't food.

"Dada?"

He looked over at Chloe, who was daintily eating what was left of her banana. "What is it, Chlo?"

She sent him her sweetest smile. "Fall down, go boom again?"

"Not on your life," he muttered balefully.

Unperturbed, she nodded. "'Kay."

Why the hell, he wondered, as he headed down the hall, did everyone seem to be happy but him?

Jessy stood in the moonlit kitchen. Her back to the counter, she dipped a spoon directly into the container of mint chocolate chip ice cream. Taking her time, she lifted it to her mouth and slid the icy treat onto her tongue.

She sighed with pleasure. It tasted terrific. Smooth, sweet, cold and creamy.

Comfort in a box.

She sighed. She couldn't remember the last time she'd felt driven to get out of bed in the middle of the night to drown her troubles in ice cream.

Well actually, maybe she could, she admitted, cursing the Goody Two-shoes part of her that insisted on being scrupulously honest. It had been almost exactly eight years ago, when Shane and Marissa had announced their engagement. She'd eaten enough ice cream that summer to raise the stock price of several ice-cream companies, and personally insure the continued employment of an entire herd of dairy cows. She'd also gained twenty-five pounds.

Suffice it to say, it had been a miserable summer.

Of course, this situation was nothing like that one, she was quick to assure herself. Then she'd been so in love with Shane she'd been convinced she would never love anyone else.

Now she knew better. She knew that a wounded heart did eventually recover. And that there were other men in the world besides Shane Wyatt. True, she'd never felt as intensely for anyone else as she once had for him, but that didn't mean anything. When the time came and she met Mr. Right, she would.

Shane, she told herself firmly as she ate another spoonful of ice cream, was Mr. Wrong. And—despite the way her emotions had been all over the place lately—she was not in love with him.

Not after the way he'd behaved today.

Her mouth tightened as she remembered. The man had been totally impossible. After he'd had his shower, he'd decided to fix his own breakfast, just as if she hadn't offered to feed him half an hour earlier. Then he'd announced he was going to pass on their planned trip to the grocery store, claiming he had some things he had to take care of. Whatever the things were, he'd finished them in time to be ensconced on the couch watching the Mariner's game when she returned. To his credit, he'd insisted on carrying in the groceries, but he'd also been distant and monosyllabic.

The day had gone downhill from there. Shane had snapped at Chloe when he'd discovered her tearing the pages out of his new copy of *Sports Illustrated*. And he'd waited until the last minute to inform Jessy he wasn't in the mood for spaghetti, when he'd known all day that was what she'd planned to make for dinner. When later she'd prevailed on him to take Chloe to feed the ducks, he'd had the nerve to act as if it were somehow her fault when he fell in the lake. He'd been testy the rest of the evening, then acted offended when she'd announced she was going to bed early.

Jessy pursed her lips. She was willing to concede the morning had started off poorly. Nobody liked to get knocked to the floor, especially before they had their first cup of coffee. And she hadn't missed his very male reaction to having her on top of him.

Still, as much as she'd love to think that at least part of his problem was sexual frustration—misery loved company, after all—she was more inclined to write his arousal off as just a guy thing. Growing up with an older brother, she'd learned early on that the male libido was much more immediate and considerably less discriminating than the female.

Which was too bad, she thought glumly. Because despite his seeming indifference to her, she couldn't shake the conviction that Shane needed her. And no matter

how badly he behaved, her feelings for him kept growing. It wasn't love, of course. But she couldn't deny that
she still felt strongly—

"Jess?"

She gave a violent start as the recessed lights overhead
snapped on and she saw the object of her thoughts standing in the doorway. Squeezing her eyes shut against the
sudden flood of light—and the truly awesome sight of
Shane dressed in nothing more than a pair of navy silk
boxers—she swallowed a groan.

What had she done to deserve this? When she'd
wanted Shane around, he'd been more elusive than snow
in July. But now, when all she wanted was some time
to think, he popped up like a bad case of hives.

Still, it was doubtful he was going to leave just because she willed him to. And, on the plus side, there was
no way he could possibly know what she'd been thinking. All she had to do was stay calm and try to act
normal and she'd get through this, just as she had everything else.

She took a deep breath and opened her eyes. Blinking
at the sudden glare, she got a second shock as her vision
cleared.

Shane's gaze was all over her. Like liquid silver, it
slid down the deep V neck of her sleep shirt and kept
on going. Although she knew it was impossible, it was
as if he could see right through the soft, blue fabric to
the swell of her breasts, the flare of her hips, the juncture
of her thighs.

A burst of heat exploded low in her stomach. She felt
her breasts tighten and she knew, without looking down,
that her nipples had hardened into telltale points. Just as
she suddenly knew that she'd been wrong about Shane.
Whatever else he might be, he wasn't indifferent to her.

She could see the intensity of his feelings in the sudden tension straining his face. And in the way his hands were balled into fists. And she could hear it in his voice as he abruptly shifted his gaze from her body to her face and said roughly, "What are you doing up?"

Heaven help her, but for a moment she almost blurted out the truth and said, *Thinking of you.* She swallowed. "Having some ice cream."

He gave her a narrow look, then headed toward the cabinets to her right. "In the dark?" He opened a cupboard and got a glass, his movements short and jerky.

She looked down at the container and shrugged. "It tastes better without distractions. What about you?"

"What about me?"

"What are you doing up?"

"I was thirsty." As if to prove it, he filled the glass with water from the tap, drained it and set it on the counter.

Jessy decided she didn't buy it. If what he'd wanted was a drink, the master bathroom was a lot closer to his bedroom than the kitchen. Her pulse quickened as she realized it was another sign that there was a lot more going on with him than he wanted her to know.

And she suddenly knew she wasn't going to let it go. If nothing else, they needed to clear the air.

"Shane?"

"What?"

Again, his gaze raked over her, and she felt a rush of awareness she was helpless to stop. "I think we need to talk."

He shook his head, already on his way out of the room. "Not now, Jess. It's late."

"But—"

"Man, I'm beat. I'll see you in the morning." Before

she could voice a protest, he disappeared into the darkness of the hall.

Jessy stood rooted to the spot. For an instant she couldn't believe that she'd finally screwed up the courage to talk, only to have him walk out on her.

Then the reality set in. She wasn't sure whether to laugh, cry—or commit an act of mayhem.

One thing was for sure. She didn't have to worry about gaining weight. She'd definitely lost her appetite.

Eight

Shane leaned back in the deck chair. Casually dressed in a white cotton shirt open at the throat and a pair of old jeans, he stretched out his legs, closed his eyes and raised his face to the sky. The afternoon was close to perfect. The sun was strong, while the breeze blowing in off the lake kept it from being too hot. He gave a heartfelt sigh.

He'd had a productive morning. He'd gone for a long run, dictated instructions for Jeffrey regarding the upcoming work week, then gone into town to take care of some personal errands.

The best part was, he'd been able to accomplish it all without any more uncomfortable encounters with Jessy. Somehow, except for the most cursory of exchanges, they'd managed to avoid each other for the bulk of the day.

Which was just fine with him. When it came to his

best friend's little sister, he'd had about all he could take. It had been one damn thing after another all weekend, from her clothes—or the lack of them, he corrected himself grimly, recalling that skimpy little V neck thing she'd had on in the kitchen last night—to her persistent cheerfulness, which by the end of yesterday had threatened to drive him stark, stirring crazy.

Well, congratulations. The way you acted in the kitchen last night appears to have taken care of that.

His jaw bunched as he staunchly refused to acknowledge a wave of something that felt remarkably like guilt. Still, he couldn't seem to stop himself from remembering his and Jessy's only longer-than-a-minute exchange earlier today. He'd been coming in from his run; she'd had Chloe on her hip and had been on her way to meet a real estate agent, or so she said. She'd been polite and distant, everything he'd been telling himself for a month that he wanted.

And he hadn't liked it. He hadn't liked it at all.

But then, that shouldn't be such a big surprise, given that lately he didn't seem to know if he was coming or going. Just last week he'd been confident that he could handle his attraction to her. Now, a mere handful of days later, the only thing he wanted to handle…was her.

It was a galling admission. As was his suspicion that last night he'd done less than a first-rate job of hiding his feelings. His only consolation was that he still didn't think Jess had a clue how close he'd come to losing control.

He did. Try as he might—and God knew, he'd tried—he couldn't forget how, for a few agonizing seconds as he walked across the kitchen, it had been touch-and-go whether he went for a glass, or her. He'd wanted to lift her onto the counter, run his hands under her nightshirt and touch her all over.

And that was just for starters.

But he hadn't. He didn't know whether it was courage or just plain stubbornness, but he'd refused to give in to the need that had been riding him. Instead he'd found the strength to do the right thing and walk away and that was what mattered. All he had to do now was keep to himself for the rest of the day and he ought to be okay. Tomorrow he'd go back to work, which would give them both some breathing room, and by tomorrow night, everything should be back to normal.

And if it isn't, hotshot?

Scowling, he scooted lower in the chair. If it wasn't, he'd leave. He'd make another trip to Dallas. Or go check out his California accounts. Where he went didn't matter. But wherever he chose, he'd stay there until he was damn sure he had himself under control.

With that decided, some of the tension drained out of him. Feeling nominally better, he took a deep breath and tried to relax, consciously loosening his muscles, which were strung tight. He yawned, then yawned again, a real jawbreaker. Damn, but he was tired. Of course, that wasn't surprising given that he'd spent most of the night tossing and turning.

He was just starting to drift off to sleep when the sound of the latch on the patio gate being raised penetrated his consciousness. Curious, he opened his eyes a slit, looked over—and got a jolt.

It was Jessy. Or, to be more precise, someone who looked like Jessy would if she were going to star on…"Baywatch."

Her hair was wet and her feet were bare. And the rest of her—the smooth golden skin, the long limbs and slender curves—was barely covered by a one-piece, electric blue, racing-style swimsuit.

The blood started to slam through Shane's veins. He sat up, suddenly wide-awake.

The movement caught her attention. She looked up as she closed the gate and her gaze quickly grew shuttered. "Hi." Freeing the towel that was slung around her neck, she used it to blot the ends of her hair.

"Where," he said slowly, "have you been?"

She sent him another brief glance, then lowered her arms and wrapped the towel sarong-style around her slender hips. "Swimming."

"In the lake?"

Her mouth curved in a sardonic smile. "No, Shane. In Chloe's wading pool. I can't imagine how you missed me."

Scowling, he came to his feet. "It's not funny."

"So? Nothing is with you."

The observation hit its mark. His whole body went tight—a state that wasn't helped as the breeze picked up, rippling the towel and causing her nipples to tighten. "Your note said you'd put Chloe down for her nap and were going to your room to read," he growled. Stupid him. When he'd returned from running errands, he'd just naturally assumed Jessy was where she said she'd be.

"I did. But I changed my mind. I decided I needed some exercise. All right?"

"Hell, no, it's not all right. You shouldn't go swimming without telling somebody where you're going. Hell, you probably shouldn't go alone, period."

Her eyes rounded in disbelief. "You're not serious."

"It's not safe."

"For heaven's sake. I'm not a child."

He could see that. Boy, could he see that, thanks to

her clinging swimsuit and the fact that at some point he'd closed the distance between them and was now standing no more than an arm's length away. "Yeah? Well, as long as you're living in my house, I have every right to—"

"What? Tell me what to do?" She stared at him in amazement. "I don't think so, Shane," she said, her voice suddenly clipped.

He felt a muscle tick to life in his jaw. "You're my responsibility—"

"I most certainly am not." She shook her head as if she couldn't believe he'd had the nerve to say what he had. Then she took a deep breath and an obvious grip on her temper and said, in an insultingly reasonable tone, "Look, this is getting us nowhere and I'm starting to get chilled. So if you'll excuse me..." She took a step toward the sliding glass door.

Shane stepped into her path. He knew he was behaving badly, but he couldn't seem to rein himself in. "Why the hell do you always have to be so damn polite?" he demanded, apropos of nothing.

She stopped short. "Somebody has to be."

"What does that mean?"

"It means *you're* impossible. I don't know what you want."

"Don't you, Jessy? Don't you really?" She was so close he could smell the sun on her skin and it was making him crazy.

"No. And even if I did, it wouldn't matter. Because you don't seem to want anything from me."

"You're wrong," he said flatly.

"Oh, really? Then prove it," she challenged, trying to brush past him.

It was the last straw. "You got it." He reached out

and clasped her bare shoulder, knowing instinctively he'd made a mistake the minute he touched her. Even so, he didn't back off. "What I want is *this*." Without further warning, he tugged her close, lowered his head and claimed her mouth for his own.

She stood rigid in his arms for all of half a second. Then a shudder went through her and she thrust her hands in his hair and crowded against him, rocking him briefly back on his heels. "Yes," she said fiercely as his lips slanted against hers. "Oh, yes…"

Lord, but she tasted sweet. Shane didn't think he'd ever get enough. He molded his mouth to hers, feeling a fierce gratification as her lips immediately parted and she kissed him back. He slid his hands up her arms, across the top of her silky shoulders and up her neck to cup her face in his hands. Stroking the fine line of her jaw with his thumbs, he pressed kiss after hungry kiss to her moist, yielding lips.

"Don't stop," she murmured, her head falling back for the brand of his mouth. "Don't stop, don't stop…"

Muttering a reassurance, he deepened the angle of the kiss.

After countless heated minutes, she let loose of his hair and slid her hands down the column of his neck. She began to work the buttons free of his shirt. "I need…I want…I have to touch you…"

"Yeah—" His response was nearly lost in the explosion of his breath as she dragged his shirttail free and ran her hands up his sides to his chest. Fingers outspread, she stroked her palms over his pecs and brushed his nipples with her thumbs. "Oh…" she breathed against his mouth. "Oh," she whispered again as her fingertips found the arrow of black hair that bisected his abdomen.

She followed it down, circling his navel with her index finger.

The heel of her hand brushed against the rigid bulge in his jeans. Shane couldn't contain a strangled sound. He pushed her hands away, yanked loose the towel encircling her hips and tossed it away. Then he wrapped an arm around her waist and began to walk blindly backward, drawing her with him until he bumped into the screen door. He reached back and impatiently shoved it open, then stumbled over the threshold and guided her with him into the family room. Grunting as he bumped into an end table, he maneuvered them to the couch, then changed his mind and started to pull her down with him to the floor.

"Wait," Jessy said breathlessly, keeping him upright as she searched for the brass button at the top of his jeans.

Someplace in the back of her mind the voice of reason was urging her to caution. *Slow down,* it whispered. *Things are moving too fast. Maybe you should talk first, find out where things stand...*

She refused to listen. She'd waited for Shane for so long, waited and wished and prayed for this to happen. She wasn't so far gone that she thought this was going to solve all their problems, or even answer all her questions, but it was a start. A start she didn't want to delay.

She finally found the button. Impatiently she wrenched it free, then located the tab of his zipper and tugged. It gave with a satisfying rasp of sound, and she quickly hooked her fingers in his waistband and shoved. His jeans slid down and hit the rug, taking his boxers with them. His shirt followed in short order.

"Jessy—"

"Shh." She stared at him. From the strong curve of

his jaw, to the muscled planes of his stomach, to the rampant thrust of his virility, he was magnificent. For a moment, it was hard to believe he was really here, like this, with her. She reached out, needing to touch him. "You're beautiful," she whispered. She knew it wasn't a term that was usually applied to men, but in his case it fit.

His gray eyes turned so dark they appeared almost black. Reaching out, he molded her against him, caressed the sides of her breasts, then ran his hands down over her waist and her hips. "And you feel like hot satin," he said roughly as his lips again found her mouth.

She opened for his tongue, unable to stop a gasp as he worked his fingers under the swimsuit's elasticized leg openings, closed his hands on her bare flesh and rocked her against him. The lower part of the suit was still slightly damp, but she hadn't realized that she was cold until she felt the heat of his hands.

She arched her back and he promptly took advantage of her position. Releasing her mouth, he bent his dark head and took her nipple in his mouth. His tongue probed, lashing the distended tip. Not until she was twisting restlessly in his arms did he clamp down and begin to suck, his mouth wet and hot despite the thin nylon barrier.

The pleasure was intense. Jessy could feel it curling through her, a ribbon of throbbing heat that led straight to the heart of her sex. Her hands fluttered against his shoulders. "Shane! Make love to me. Now."

Slowly he straightened. His eyes searched hers for a second. She gazed back, and from somewhere she found the strength to smile. "Please?"

"Ah, Jess." Breathing hard, he took a half step back

and with fingers that trembled, he hooked his thumbs under her shoulder straps. In one quick motion, he peeled the swimsuit to her knees, then straightened and considered her.

He lost it. Clasping her hands, he tugged her to the floor and rolled her beneath him, the fierce look of need on his face better than any spoken compliment. She barely had time to brace before he spread her thighs, guided himself home and thrust.

She bucked as he filled her, her body arching as her swollen, tender sex nearly overloaded with sensation. She squeezed her eyes shut, shocked at the raw pleasure of having him inside her, so big, so hard, so hot.

She pleased him, too. "Oh damn you're tight," he groaned.

She reached up and clutched blindly at his shoulders, whimpering as he drew back so far he was almost outside her, then drove forward again. She'd never felt like this before. Her whole body was on fire, a fire fed by the press of his chest against her aching nipples, the fine prickle of the hair on his legs against her tender skin, the surging power of him between her thighs.

She opened her eyes and found he was watching her, his gaze intense. "Shane..." she gasped, a little frightened by the feeling building steadily inside her.

"Not yet," he groaned, his face strained. "Hold on, sweetheart, hold on—"

She couldn't. As he flexed his hips in a heavy surge, a dam seemed to burst. Pleasure rolled through her, so extreme it almost hurt. She cried out, her body bowing as she convulsed around him, hot and squeezing; then she cried out again as he leaned down and claimed her mouth in a carnal, openmouthed kiss. He thrust again, rocking them both. A low moan tore from his throat and his whole body shuddered as wave after wave of pleasure seemed to jolt through him.

Moments later, he collapsed against her, sobbing for breath. Jessy cradled him in her arms, welcoming his heavy weight as he buried his face in the crook of her neck. Tenderness, joy and contentment washed through her, along with another emotion, fiercer and more overwhelming than all the rest.

For the barest instant, she resisted. Yet in her heart she knew it was hopeless. There was no longer any denying it.

Smoothing her hands down Shane's back, she rested her cheek against his cool, dark hair, and finally gave herself over to the truth.

She loved him. She always had, and she always would.

Although it took a while, Shane's breathing eventually evened out. As his body quieted, his mind began to clear, and he realized that he was lying in a pool of sunlight, that the rug beneath his knees felt surprisingly soft, that the house was so quiet he could hear the soft sigh of the breeze outside.

He could feel Jessy's hands gently stroking his back.

He felt the first stirring of uneasiness.

What the hell had just happened? Never before had his need for sex been so…urgent. Never, not even as a randy teenager, had he been so wildly out of control. And never, ever, had he continued to feel such intense desire for a woman when he was still weak and trembling from his last climax.

Yet his sex continued to feel hot, heavy and aching. And despite a harsh inner voice that kept insisting he'd made a huge mistake by making love to Jessy in the first place, he had an overwhelming urge to rise up, taste the sweetness of her mouth and lose himself inside her a second time.

But he didn't. Instead he clenched his teeth and forced himself to lie still, not to react even as she began to massage his back with her fingertips and a fresh rush of need washed through him.

Mercifully, after a few minutes, her fingers stilled. "Shane? Are you okay?"

God help them both, but he wasn't. He needed some time and space to put what had just happened into perspective. He needed to think, to figure out how best to explain that nothing could ever come of the attraction between them. He needed—

Knock it off, Wyatt, the little voice in his head said contemptuously. *You chose this course, even though you've known all along that Jessy wasn't for you. Now you have to live with the consequences.*

He took a deep breath, recognizing the truth when he heard it. Just as he suddenly knew that no matter how he felt about what he and Jess had just shared, he didn't want to hurt her. She deserved better. Better than this and better than him.

"Shane?" she said again, starting to sound worried.

Taking a firm grip on his seesawing emotions, he rocked back, disengaging their bodies. He rolled to one side, braced himself on one elbow, looked down at her—and lied. "I'm fine, Jess. Why?"

She studied him, her clear blue eyes concerned as they played over his face. "Because for a man who just made love, you seem a little...tense."

He shrugged, but he could see from her expression that she wasn't buying it.

"What's the matter?" she asked softly.

He sighed—and lied again. "I'm sorry. It's just...everything happened too fast. I should have gone slower. And not been so rough."

Her expression changed, going from concerned to amazed in a heartbeat. "But you weren't. Trust me. It was perfect." A look came over her face, a sort of shy amazement he'd never seen from her before. With a candor that stabbed his heart, she added, "I didn't know it could be like that."

Neither had he. But he wasn't about to admit it—for both their sakes. He shook his head. "That still doesn't make it right."

She considered a moment, then caught him by surprise. "All right. So make it up to me."

"What?"

Her clear blue eyes glinted mischievously. "Do it again." Craning her neck, she glanced briefly downward. "I think you're up to it."

For the first time in his life, he cursed the anatomy that made his desires so obvious—and made the truth impossible to avoid. He sighed, searching for just the right words. "Jess, listen. I'm not going to lie to you. Yeah, I want you. But that doesn't mean it's a good idea. For either of us."

She went very still. "You want to be a little more specific?"

"Sure. Bottom line, you and me, together, like this— it's not going to work."

"I...see." She looked at him for several impossibly long seconds, then abruptly sat up. After a quick look around, she snagged his discarded shirt, slipped it on and stood, flipping her shiny honey-colored hair over the up-turned collar. She moved a few steps away. "I don't suppose you'd like to explain why?'' she said, holding the shirt closed with her hands.

He forced himself to ignore the prurient part of him that was sorry to see her cover up and concentrated on climbing to his feet and pulling on his jeans. ''Because I'm not ready for anything permanent. I don't know if I'll ever be. And I don't want to hurt you.''

''Ah.'' She fell silent, apparently considering his words. After a moment, she said carefully, ''You know, Shane, as much as I appreciate you worrying about me, don't you think you're being a little...presumptuous?''

''How do you mean?''

''I mean that I don't recall asking you for a lifetime commitment or anything.''

He stared at her in surprise. He wasn't sure what he'd expected her to say, but that definitely wasn't it. And though he knew it wasn't fair, suddenly he felt frustrated—with himself and her and the whole situation. For some reason he didn't care to examine, the thought that she might not care about him at all was almost as upsetting as the idea that she did. ''So what are you saying? That you were just after a one-night stand? Or—'' he had another, even more disturbing thought ''—was this just another one of your teenage fantasies?''

She instantly shook her head. ''No. Of course not. What I'm saying is that I'm an adult. And I don't need you to make decisions for me—or protect me from myself. Why can't we just have some fun, enjoy the summer—and each other—and see what comes? Heck, maybe in a few weeks we'll be sick of each other.''

Shane seriously doubted that. But as for the other...

He rocked back on his heels and turned away, his thoughts in a quandary. Maybe she was right, he thought slowly, turning over what she'd said in his mind. Maybe he had jumped the gun by assuming that a relationship between them could only end badly. After all, she was a hundred percent correct about one thing—she *was* an adult. And, God knew, so far she hadn't behaved the way he'd expected when it came to anything else. As a matter of fact, hadn't he found himself thinking on more than one occasion that when it came to the important stuff, she tended to act more like a guy?

Still… He brought his gaze back to her. "If I say no, that it just won't work, what then?"

She considered. "I guess we try to go back to the way things were. Although—" She hesitated.

"What?"

She shrugged. "I think it would be awfully hard."

He looked at her. Framed by the afternoon sunlight, her hair and skin gleamed like gold, while her eyes were bluer than the summer sky. Her cheeks were pink from his beard, her mouth was pouty and swollen and he could see a tantalizing V of cleavage above the stark white edges of his shirt. And then there were her legs, her long, beautiful, incredibly sexy legs…

Going back wouldn't be hard: it would be impossible. Yet the only other alternative was for her to leave—and how could he do that to Chloe?

"All right," he said slowly. "We can try it your way. As long as you understand this doesn't mean we're a couple, or joined at the hip—and that there are no guarantees about the future." He hesitated, struck by how cold, how calculated—how selfish—he sounded. Yet it was for her own good, he reminded himself. She'd be a hell of a lot better off once she realized the kind of man he really was.

She stepped close and lightly laid her hand on his arm.

"Relax. I'm a big girl. I promise I have no desire to turn you into my personal escort service, okay?"

"Jess—"

"It'll be all right, Shane. Really." She smiled, warm and easy as always, and some of his tension drained away.

Unable to help himself, he reached out and slid his hand under the warm curtain of her hair, then stroked the satiny skin behind her ear. "Maybe. Although you realize Bailey's gonna kill me if he ever finds out?"

A faint smile touched her lips. "I'll protect you," she said solemnly. She clasped her hands around his neck, leaving the shirt to fall open.

"Promise?"

"Absolutely."

"I'm going to hold you to that." He ducked his head and began to kiss the tender flesh under her jaw. "How long do you think before Chloe wakes up?"

She arched her neck for his mouth. "I don't know. Half an hour?" Her voice was low and aching.

"Long enough." He swung her up into his arms and carried her off to his bed.

Nine

Fremont Bluff lay along the eastern shore of Lake Winston.

As recently as ten years earlier, it had been *the* place for local teens to bring their dates for a little extracurricular activity, due to its seclusion and its spectacular view of the water.

Now, suburbia had encroached and houses like Shane's ringed the lake. The old make-out place was long gone. In its place was a family park, with picnic and play areas along the bluff and a winding ramp cut into the hill that led to a dock and the beach below.

The only thing that remained the same was the view, Jessy thought, gazing admiringly to the west where the fiery orange disk of the sun hung in the early-evening sky. Through some optical trick, fingers of light seemed to stream from it to the snaggle-toothed tops of the Olympic Mountains, turning them purple and crimson.

The same light danced in golden arcs across the blue-green surface of the lake.

It was almost as nice to look at as Shane, she decided, shifting her gaze to the clean lines of his profile as he sat beside her at one of the park's many picnic tables. Not that she was prejudiced or anything.

Nope, not her. Besotted was more like it.

Yet, to her credit, that was just on the inside. On the outside, she thought she'd done a pretty good job holding the line these two weeks at appearing only moderately infatuated.

Which only went to show how really far gone she was.

Because if it was anyone but Shane, pride alone would have dictated that she walk away from the situation. She was long past an age when she found anything admirable or attractive about unrequited love. And she had more than enough self-respect to believe she deserved more than just a casual affair.

But the bottom line was, she loved him. And she wasn't willing to let him retreat behind the wall he'd built for himself, thanks to whatever it was that had hurt him so terribly.

Besides, she didn't believe Shane was capable of a solely physical relationship. If he was, why hadn't he had one before now? And why had he tried to break things off between them practically before they started?

Perhaps she was deluding herself, but she believed it was because he did care for her, maybe more than he realized—surely more than he'd ever admit. The evidence was there in the hunger of his lovemaking, the way he held her tight in his sleep, the way he was starting to remember how to laugh. Although it wasn't much, it was a start, something to build on. She wasn't looking for guarantees. All she wanted was a chance.

She let out her breath, inadvertently disrupting their companionable silence. Shane gave a slight start and looked away from the lake, where a sleek jet boat was pulling a pair of water-skiers, to focus on her. "You okay?"

She smiled, and put her errant thoughts out of her mind, determined to enjoy their time together. "Yeah. I think I ate too much, though." They'd stopped for dinner at a local fast-food joint on the way. "My eyes were bigger than my stomach. As usual."

"I know what you mean." He patted his lean stomach. "If I keep eating the way I have lately, I won't be able to snap my jeans."

She made a face. "Oh, please. Give me a break. Unlike the rest of us mere mortals, you don't have an ounce of fat on you. Anywhere."

Their eyes met, and just like that, awareness simmered between them. Looking into his handsome face, Jessy was reminded of all the intimacies they'd recently shared. She could see from Shane's expression that he was remembering, too. She reached out and closed her hand around his.

After a moment's hesitation, his fingers curled around hers. As if that was all the closeness he could handle, however, he looked back at the lake. "As nice as this is, I'm sure you're ready for a night out." He hesitated a second, then added, "I'm sorry we couldn't get a baby-sitter."

Despite his offhand tone, there was something in his voice that made her think he expected her to complain. "I told you it's no big deal. Dinner was fine, Chloe's having fun—" they both glanced over at the toddler, who was sitting fifty feet away in the sandbox, happily playing trucks in an enclosed play area with a pair of little boys she'd befriended ''—and the company's first-rate.'' She gave his hand a squeeze. ''Besides, it's way too nice an evening to spend it sitting inside somewhere.''

He glanced at her, then away, but not before she saw the look on his face. ''What is it?''

He shrugged. ''Sometimes I just don't get you.''

''What's to get?''

''You're just so damn...easy.''

''Hmm.'' She pretended to consider. ''I'm going to assume that's a compliment.''

As she'd hoped it would, the comment brought his head around and put a faint gleam of amusement into his gray eyes. ''Very funny. You know what I mean.''

The thing was, she did. She understood that he didn't expect things to go well. Which just strengthened her determination to prove him wrong—and do whatever she had to to bring a smile to his face.

For that reason, she again deliberately chose not to take him seriously. ''Hey, what can I say?'' she said, straight-faced. ''That I know I'm terrific? Or would you rather I just congratulate you for your good taste?''

He snorted. ''You're incorrigible.''

''I know. Aren't you glad?'' She grinned.

Almost reluctantly, he grinned back.

A flash of motion in the corner of her eye captured her attention. Suddenly alert, she looked over at Chloe and her newfound friends, then sighed as she saw that all three kids had removed their shoes and socks, filled them with sand and were throwing them at each other. ''Uh-oh,'' she murmured.

''I'll second that,'' Shane said.

She switched her gaze to him and found he was looking at her expectantly, as if waiting for her to do something. She shook her head. "No way. It's your turn."

"What?"

"Hey, I've already played referee twice tonight. Besides, I think those little boys will respond better to a male authority figure."

"Those little boys would respond better to *any* authority figure," he said with a pointed look at their teenage baby-sitter, who was sitting across the way, giggling away as she talked into a cell phone. With a resigned sigh, he stood. "Okay, I'll go. But I hope you realize what a come-down this is."

"How so?" Despite his put-upon air, she thought she could see a gleam of amusement in his eyes.

"The last time I was at this bluff, I was on a mission to unhook Mary Jane Feenamen's bra. Now I'm stuck with toddler patrol."

She made a *tsk*ing sound. "I hate to break it to you, but if you're looking for sympathy, bringing up a former conquest isn't going to do it."

"How do you know she was a conquest?"

"Because you're too egotistical to mention it otherwise."

To her delight, he actually laughed. Bemused by the wonderful sound, she watched him walk away, admiring the long line of his back and the way his snug black jeans emphasized his narrow hips and tight masculine fanny.

He reached the sandbox and stooped down. He talked to the children for a minute or two, then said something that made all three of them turn, stare at her and nod earnestly, before turning back to him. Like little angels, they each dumped the sand out of their shoes, shook out their socks, then waited patiently for Shane to help them put the items back on.

Once finished, he straightened and walked back to her, a satisfied look on his face. "There." He sat down on the bench beside her, his thigh a warm pressure against her leg as he reached casually for his soft drink. "Happy?"

"Impressed is more like it. Wow. What did you say to get them to cooperate like that?"

"Oh, nothing," he said blandly, obviously pleased with himself. "I just told them that if they were good, kept all their clothes on and didn't throw sand, you'd take them on the merry-go-round in a little while."

"Why—you bum!" Laughing, she tried to sock him on the shoulder but he caught her hand and held it against his chest. "I'll make you pay later, you know," she threatened, even as something inside her melted when she felt the steady beat of his heart beneath her palm.

Satisfaction—and something very male—gleamed in his gray eyes. "I'm counting on it."

"You were right about getting her into her pajamas at the park," Shane said to Jessy's back as he carried Chloe's limp little form down the darkened hallway toward her bedroom. "She's really out."

Jessy looked at him over her shoulder. "Keeping up with those boys was hard work." She led the way into the toddler's room, her path illuminated by the bunny-shaped night-light set into an outlet in the far wall.

"Yeah, but she held her own." He waited as Jessy lowered the crib railing, then gently shifted Chloe into the cradle of his arms.

"Of course, she did." A smile in her voice, Jessy

reached for the soft blue blanket folded at the end of the mattress. "She may look like a little angel, but she's got one heck of a stubborn streak. But then, I guess she comes by it naturally. She is, after all, your daughter."

He flinched at her well-meaning comment, only to give a start when she straightened and leaned companionably against him. Offset by her comforting warmth, the expected moment of anguish never materialized.

Unaware of his sudden inner turmoil, she slid her arm around his waist and gave him a gentle hug. "She's a wonderful little girl, Shane. You two are lucky to have each other."

"Yeah," he said slowly. "I guess we are." He glanced down at the baby in his arms. Her eyes were shut, her Cupid's bow lips parted as her head rested trustingly against the bend of his arm. His heart squeezed, but not in a bad way. Perplexed, but afraid to dwell on it for fear of deliberately stirring up all the usual, painful feelings, he bent down and brushed her petal soft cheek with a kiss.

Straightening, he leaned over and carefully laid her down on the mattress, then stepped back to give Jessy room to cover her with the blanket and slide the crib rail back into place.

"It won't be long before she's ready for a real bed," she murmured as they tiptoed out of the room.

He made a noncommittal answer as he waited for her to close the door. Although he knew that at some point he was going to have to figure out what had just happened with Chloe, he wasn't going to do it now. There would be plenty of time for thinking…later. Now was for him and Jessy—and for finally taking care of the desire that had grown steadily over the past couple of hours.

His mouth quirked ruefully as he conceded the irony of the latter. After all, it wasn't as if he'd exactly been celibate the past few weeks, he acknowledged. Sure, he'd started off in great shape, determined to reestablish some distance, to make it clear to Jess that he had himself firmly back under control and that he'd meant what he said about limiting their involvement.

Yet right from the start, his body had refused to cooperate. While his intellect warned that it would be wise to take things slowly, his libido found everything about Jessy an aphrodisiac, from her scent to the sound of her laughter. Perfectly innocent things excited him, from the sight of her brushing her hair to the feel of her fingers grazing his palm when she handed him a cup of coffee. Right or wrong, she turned him on just by breathing. And no matter how sternly he vowed to keep his hands—and everything else—to himself, he'd still found himself waking up in her bedroom every single morning for the past two weeks.

A faint, self-deprecating smile tugged at his mouth. He had to admit that in the beginning he'd expected that once his itch was scratched, it would at least diminish, if not go away entirely. But instead it just kept getting worse, like a bad case of poison ivy. He ought to be alarmed. And he probably would be…if all his energy wasn't going into being aroused.

Jessy touched her hand to his shoulder. "Shane? Are you in there?"

Her wry inquiry put an end to his musing. "Yeah. Didn't you just say something about beds?" He drew her into his arms.

"As a matter of fact, I did."

Although they were standing in the shadows beyond the spill of light from the family room, he saw the amusement tug at the corners of her mouth as he said solemnly, "I have one, you know."

"Really? How interesting."

He pulled her a little closer. "It could be."

She clasped her hands around his neck and pretended to consider. "Maybe. But then again, that undercover cop show I like is on TV tonight—"

"Hey, I can do undercover work." She gave a satisfying little gasp as he tugged her T-shirt out of her shorts and slid his hands under the hem. "All I need is the right incentive."

"Such as?"

Her back felt warm and silky. "Oh, I don't know. How about killer underwear?"

"I can do that."

"You can?"

"Absolutely. Come with me—" she took a half step back, forcing him to slide his hands free of her shirt, took his hand and started toward his bedroom "—and I'll show you."

Shane's whole body tightened. With Marissa, sex had always been serious, intense and totally his responsibility. Although his own reaction surprised him, he found Jessy's willingness to take the initiative a major turn-on.

Bemused, he entered his bedroom a step behind her. The drapes were open and he was peripherally aware that beyond the French doors, the lake lay as still and glassy as a giant reflecting pool, its surface glittering with the milky light of a full, summer moon.

Then he forgot all about the view as Jessy turned, slid her hands into his hair and covered his mouth with her own.

He swallowed a groan. After the past two weeks, a mere kiss should have seemed old hat. Instead the light pressure of her lips and the unhurried brush of her fingertips along his jaw were enough to hollow his stomach and set off a heavy throbbing in his loins.

He reached for her.

She instantly pulled back and scooted out of range. "No. Not yet," she said softly.

"Jess." The single word was full of need—and warning.

She shook her head, her hair gleaming like silver in the moonlight. "Patience," she advised, a smile in her voice. "I thought we were working on that incentive." Taking a shallow breath, she crossed her arms, reached for the hem of her shirt and drew it over her head to reveal a sheer, plunging, black-as-the-night bra.

His breath whistled soundlessly through his teeth. Through some feat of engineering, the thing made her full, pretty breasts look like some sort of pagan offering. He stretched out his hands.

This time she didn't move, except to shiver as he cupped her fullness in his palms and dragged his thumbs over her distended nipples. "Oh," she exclaimed breathlessly.

"You like that?"

"Mmm." She moistened her lips and leaned slightly forward.

Her breasts plumped in his hands and for a second he thought he was going to lose it right there. Gritting his teeth, he leaned down, buried his face in her softness and again slowly rubbed her nipples with his thumbs, rewarded as a quiver went through her. He kissed the shadowy V of her cleavage and the delicate notch at her collarbone, then slid his lips up her throat, along the delicate point of her chin and over her mouth for a probing, carnal kiss. Her lips parted eagerly for his tongue.

When he lifted his head, they were both breathing hard, but when he tried to draw her to the bed, she once again resisted. "Wait." Tossing her hair back over her shoulders, she stepped out of her sandals and peeled off her shorts. When she straightened, he saw that what she was wearing for panties was a sheer, barely there black satin thong that tied over her hips.

"Oh, man," he said hoarsely. "You really know how to torture a guy." Taking her hands, he backed toward the bed, sinking down as his knees hit the foot of the mattress. "I think it's about time I return the favor." He let go of her wrists, wrapped his fingers around the back of her long, slim thighs, leaned forward and opened his mouth over her soft, satin-covered cleft.

She gasped, gripping his shoulders for balance. "Shane!"

"I know, baby. I know," he murmured, her woman's scent filling his head as he began to press long, hot kisses to her sensitive flesh. Despite her urging, he took his time, not satisfied until her body quivered with each brush of his lips and she could no longer hold back a whimper.

Shane more than understood. His own skin felt hot and damp, and his jeans were so tight that he wouldn't be surprised if he had a zipper-shaped bruise tomorrow. Yet he wasn't about to stop. Not when she tasted so sweet...

He moved his head lower, stroking her through the satin with his tongue until he felt her entire body jolt. With heady satisfaction, he sucked strongly on that single pleasure point.

Above him, Jessy's head fell back, twisting back and forth as her hands dug into his shoulders. "Oh. Oh, yes. Oh, please!" Her breathless cries of pleasure nearly did him in, but he didn't let up until suddenly, she cried out his name and her whole body went rigid.

In the next instant, she collapsed against him as if she were a house of cards and they toppled back onto the bed.

They came to rest with her on top. "Oh, Shane," she murmured, burying her face in his neck as the tension drained out of her.

He closed his eyes as her breasts pressed against his chest. Despite the urgent need that wasn't getting any better with her draped all over him, he forced himself to stay still, wanting to give her a chance to catch her breath.

His effort lasted until he felt her shift upright. Opening his eyes, he found her smiling down at him in the moonlight. "Hi," she said softly.

His control vanished like a conjurer's dream at her heavy-lidded look of satisfaction. "Damn." He ground out the word as he arched his back, reached down and ripped open his jeans. "I thought I could wait. I keep thinking I'm gonna get a grip on this…"

He snapped the thin satin ties on her panties. Yanking the scrap of material away, he urged her forward with a hand to her bottom while he steadied himself. "There, oh, there, yes, ah, Jess—" He sucked in a breath as she enveloped him, so warm, so wet, so tight. Then he gasped as she began to ride him, rising and falling, then slowly rotating her hips.

Although it wasn't easy, he reached up, found the clasp on her bra and unsnapped it. Free of constraint, her breasts spilled forward and into his hands. He cupped the warm, soft flesh, groaning as he took one pebbled nipple into his mouth, his cheeks hollowing rhythmically as he began to suckle.

Jessy made a soft inarticulate sound. He felt her bear down and felt the soft sheathing of her interior muscles contract, squeezing him in a way that made the sweat pop up on his brow. Then she gasped, arched her back and cried out, her hands clutching his biceps as a fresh wave of pleasure rocketed through her.

The breath exploded from Shane's lungs. Grabbing her hips, he held her in place as he planted his feet and thrust, again and again, until suddenly his whole body tightened, then seemed to expand with the power of his release. *"Jess!"* He was helpless to stop the low groan that was torn from his throat with each hot, jetting pulsation.

He fell back against the mattress, cradling Jessy against him as she collapsed for the second time.

Still joined together, they lay there, chests heaving, holding each other tight. When their mutual tumult finally subsided, Jessy rolled into the curve of his arm and snuggled against him. "Oh," she said breathlessly, then shocked him as she let loose with a ripple of laughter. The sound was low, husky and joyous. "That was wonderful."

Shane went still. Laughter in the bedroom had been a commodity in short supply in his previous life. Now, a flood tide of emotions washed through him. There was a torrent of affection, a powerful gush of possessiveness—and something else, something so foreign it took him a moment to identify it.

Happiness.

His throat went tight...because he knew from experience it was an emotion that couldn't last.

Ten

"**W**ant Belle to go bye-bye, too."

"I know, sweetie. Don't worry. I'll find her. She's got to be here someplace." Jessy glanced from the toddler's anxious face to her watch. If she and Chloe didn't get a move on, they were going to run smack into the middle of rush hour, which would make them late getting to Margaret's house, which in turn meant they'd hold up dinner for all the other guests.

Yet it wasn't mere politeness that made her want to hurry. Quite simply, she was looking forward to the get-together.

Although she loved the time she spent with Chloe, and there was no one she'd rather be with than Shane, it was going to be fun to see her fellow teachers and their spouses for a change.

She was looking forward to hearing what everyone had been up to so far this summer, to talking about the

upcoming school year, to showing off Chloe and to just
hanging out—to borrow one of her students' favorite
phrases.

Yet she knew it was no use trying to explain that to
Chloe. No way was the child setting foot out the door
without Belle, so she might as well quit worrying about
the time and try to concentrate on finding the darn doll.

With that in mind, she took a deep breath and forced
herself to go over her and Chloe's movements that day.
As quickly as that, it came to her. "I'll be right back,"
she told the child.

"Okeydokey," Chloe said, using her favorite new
phrase, which she had picked up from one of the boys
at the park last week.

She hurried down the hall and into the bathroom, giving a sigh of relief when she saw Belle propped on the
edge of the counter, where she'd "watched" Chloe getting her hair done earlier. Smiling, she pounced on the
errant doll and trotted back to the family room, where
she was rewarded for her effort by the sight of Chloe's
face lighting up.

"Belle!" the toddler cried, as if her plastic friend had
been missing for days instead of half an hour.

Jessy handed the baby doll over. "There she is, safe
and sound. Can we go now?"

The child beamed. "Okeydokey."

"Thank goodness." She took one last look around the
room, but she couldn't think of anything else she had to
have, so she grabbed her purse, slung the straps of
Chloe's diaper bag cum backpack over one shoulder,
then stooped down to scoop up the child.

The phone rang. "Oh, for heaven's sake!" With a
sigh—was it written somewhere that she was doomed to
spend the next hour in bumper-to-bumper traffic?—she

relinquished her hold on both bags and straightened. "I'll just be a minute, okay?" she told Chloe.

"Okeydokey," the toddler said, unperturbed.

Jessy dashed across the room and snatched up the receiver. "Hello?"

"Hi. It's me."

Her irritation vanished. "Shane," she said warmly, even as she wondered what was up. Despite the change in their relationship, he wasn't one for idle chitchat, at least not on the phone. When he called, it was usually for a specific purpose.

His next words confirmed that observation. "I just thought I'd better let you know that I'm going to be home for dinner after all."

"You are?" The last she'd heard, he had plans to go to the Mariners' game.

"Yeah. Neal Larsen, the guy with the tickets, called a little while ago to cancel. He's got some sort of family emergency."

"Oh. Well, I hope everything's okay. And I'm sorry you have to miss the game."

"No big deal. You want me to pick something up for dinner on the way home?"

"Actually I'm just on my way out the door myself."

There was the slightest pause. "You are?"

"Yeah. Margaret Keogh, one of the other sixth-grade teachers from my school, is having a barbecue. A bunch of the staff and their families are invited."

"Oh."

"I meant to tell you about it last night, but what with you getting home so late—" *and taking me straight to bed* "—I forgot."

This time, the silence on the other end of the line was

more pronounced. "I see," Shane said finally. "I assume you're taking Chloe?"

"Of course." She hesitated, then said to heck with it. Although she hadn't forgotten his stipulation that they remain free to go their own way, much less her promise that she wouldn't automatically expect him to accompany her places, surely this qualified as an exception. "You're welcome to come along."

As if he was weighing her words, there was another little silence before he said, "I'd better not. You're ready to leave, and I'm at least an hour out. You go ahead."

She swallowed her disappointment and glanced at her watch, aware the time was ticking away. "In that case I better get going before traffic gets too horrible. I left you a note, with the phone number and everything."

"Fine."

"We shouldn't be too late."

"All right."

"I hope you have a nice night."

"Yeah. You, too."

The line clicked off. Slowly Jessy replaced the receiver. She knew she was probably being overly sensitive, but toward the end there, Shane had sounded a little...curt. Troubled, she reviewed their conversation, trying to decide if what she'd heard in his voice was merely disappointment at having his plans fall apart, or if it had been something else. After all, she had broken the "rules" by asking him along. But under the circumstances, surely he wouldn't be upset....

With a sudden shrug, she decided she was probably imagining things. And if for some reason she wasn't, there would be time enough to find out what the problem was tomorrow. Right now, she had somewhere to go and people to see and she wasn't about to let some foolish, unsubstantiated worry ruin the evening.

"Come on, pumpkin." Walking back across the room, she grabbed the bags, scooped Chloe up and headed for the garage. "Let's go have some fun."

Shane pushed the lawn mower into the tool shed with a less-than-gentle shove. It was just his luck that the damn thing had chosen today to give up the ghost, turning what should have been a simple Saturday morning job into a half-day hassle. He'd made two trips to the hardware store for parts, scraped his knuckles on the engine housing, spilled oil on his shirt, and he had grass stains all over his jeans.

Come Monday morning he was hiring a lawn service, he thought darkly, stalking toward the house. Either that, or he was having the whole damn yard redone in concrete.

He yanked open the patio door. Giving an involuntary sigh of relief as a chill rush of air-conditioned air washed over him, he stepped inside—only to stiffen as he spotted Jessy seated at the kitchen counter.

"Hi," she said with a sunny smile.

Even though he knew it was unfair, his irritability increased. She just looked so clean and cool in her soft yellow shirt and her crisp white shorts, while he felt hot, sweaty and too frustrated to pretend a niceness he didn't feel. "Hey, Jess." He slid the door shut and strode toward the kitchen. Maybe a cold drink would mellow him out.

She set aside the stack of papers she'd been perusing. "Did you finally figure out what was wrong with the lawn mower?"

Now there was a subject unlikely to improve his disposition. "Yep. You were right and I was wrong," he said tightly. "Turned out it was the air filter and not the spark plug after all." He yanked open the refrigerator door, grabbed a can of cola, popped the top and took a long swallow. He knew he was being rude, but he couldn't seem to stop. He'd been bent out of shape ever since last night, due, he was quick to assure himself, to his disappointment at missing the Mariners' game.

Jessy wisely changed the subject. "Are you hungry? I made you a sandwich. It's on a plate in the fridge."

He heard the sound of her stool scraping back and twisted around. "I'll get it," he said sharply. He didn't think he could stand to be fussed over at the moment.

"Okay." She sat back down. "No problem."

He pretended not to notice the suddenly oppressive silence. Retrieving the plate, he carried it over to the far counter, stripped off the cellophane wrapper and went to get some potato chips out of the cupboard.

All right. So maybe it wasn't only missing the game that was eating at him. Maybe he was also a little bent out of shape with Jessy, thanks to the whole business of the get-together at her friend's last night. Not that he cared that she'd gone. Or even that she'd just assumed he wouldn't mind if she took Chloe. But it rankled big time that she hadn't planned on providing him with any more explanation than some pitiful note. Almost as much as it galled him that she hadn't bothered to ask him along until she'd practically been forced into it.

Yet he knew damn well there was no way he could say so—not after he'd made such a big deal about keeping their relationship free of the usual expectations, and how she wasn't to think of them as a couple. Just as he could hardly admit that when he'd said all that, he'd been thinking about her wanting more than he could give, and not the other way around.

But then, for some reason it had never occurred to him she might take him at his word and go on about her life as if he wasn't a part of it. And he sure hadn't expected that being excluded might eat at him like this.

But she had. And it did.

A sardonic smile twisted his lips. *Gee, Wyatt. Does the phrase "hoist on your own petard" ring a bell?*

"Shane?"

He looked warily over at Jessy. "What?"

"Is there a problem?"

He definitely did *not* want to have this conversation. Not now, when the little voice in his head was having a field day trying to decide whether he could best be described as a shortsighted fool or a self-centered jerk. And not with his temper already raw and his emotions bouncing around like so many rubber balls. "I don't know what you mean."

"I mean the way you've been acting lately."

"What about it?"

Her steady gaze didn't waver. "Oh, come on. You barely said a word when I got home last night. You've avoided me most of today. And every time I try to talk to you, either it's like pulling teeth or you snap at me."

"Last night I was tired," he said defensively. "Today I've been busy."

She appeared completely unimpressed. "You weren't too tired or busy to make love, not last night and not this morning."

Great. Just what he needed. Another reminder that where she was concerned his middle name was horny. "So?"

"So does this have something to do with my going to Margaret's last night?"

Leave it to Jessy to zero right in on the heart of things. "No," he said stubbornly. "Why would you think that?"

"Because of the way you're acting," she said patiently. "And because you sounded a little strained on the phone yesterday."

"No, I didn't."

"And because I'd feel bad," she persisted, "if somehow I'd hurt your feelings and didn't know it."

"Look, just forget it, okay?"

"No."

"What do you mean, *no?*"

She didn't even try to hide her exasperation. "I mean I'm not about to forget it, Shane."

"Yeah? Well, fine! The problem, if you've got to know, is that I've got the Martinson wedding to go to next weekend, and I wanted you to go with me, but you made it pretty damn clear last night, with your reluctant little last-minute invitation, that you're not interested in being seen with me!"

"What?" Her eyes went wide with amazement.

He slammed his mouth shut. Where the hell had that come from?

Not that it mattered. No matter how hotly he might try to deny it, he could see from the way the astonishment on her face was starting to fade that she was already beginning to grasp the broader implications.

Jaw set, he stared stonily at her and waited.

It didn't take long. "You really think I don't want to go to the wedding with you?"

"Just let it go, Jess."

She shook her head. "Oh, no, Shane. Not a chance. I

want to be sure I understand this. You're mad at me because I won't go to a wedding that you haven't invited me to. And the reason you know I won't go, even though you haven't asked, is because—despite the fact that you already had plans for last night, and that you made it pretty darn clear our relationship was conditional on my *not* asking you to go places—I didn't initially invite you to Margaret's. Right?''

Put like that, it sounded even more ludicrous than he'd expected. Even so, he crossed his arms over his chest, tried hard not to look as asinine as he felt and said, ''Well…yeah.''

''Ah.'' She gave him a long, indecipherable look and slowly nodded. ''I see.'' Her lips began to tremble. She tried to control it, but it got steadily worse, until finally she clapped a hand to her mouth and jerked her gaze away from his.

''Jess?'' Damn it, he couldn't stand it if he'd made her cry.

She glanced back at him and lost it. Snatching her hand from her face, she began to giggle. ''I'm sorry, Sh-Shane,'' she sputtered. ''But you have to admit—'' the giggles gave way to a full-throated chuckle ''—that it sounds pretty off-the-wall when you s-say it out loud like that.''

She thought it was funny? His emotions still roiling, he stared at her in disbelief, not sure whether to be relieved or insulted.

Yet the instant he stopped to think about it, to reflect that she was neither screaming at him nor crying, and that Marissa would have done both given a similar situation, relief won.

Still, if he knew Jessy, he wasn't entirely off the hook. His hunch was confirmed a second later as her laughter subsided. Taking a deep, calming breath, she looked over at him expectantly. "Well?"

"You really gonna make me say it?"

"Oh, absolutely."

He sighed. "Okay, then. I'm sorry—"

"No, Shane," she interrupted gently. "Not that."

He stared at her a moment, not quite sure he'd heard her right. Then, as it dawned on him what she wanted, he felt a burst of relief, bigger than the first—and a swell of affection so strong that it was a moment before he could speak. "All right," he said finally. "Would you *please* go to the wedding with me?"

She smiled. "I'd love to."

There. As easy as that, it was settled. He let out a breath he hadn't known he was holding.

Yet even as he found himself returning her smile, a little voice in his head was demanding to know what he thought he was doing.

Watch out, Wyatt, it warned. *You're getting in over your head.*

"I love weddings," Jessy said wryly, glancing at the half-dozen bridesmaids who dotted the bustling reception. To a woman, they were each attired in garish lavender organza dresses, each with a bouffant skirt, huge puffy sleeves, an elaborate sash at the waist and large purple satin bows at the neckline and hem.

She shook her head and glanced at Shane, who was seated beside her at one of the many banquettes that edged the lavish reception room. "What other occasion would prompt a bunch of no-doubt intelligent, otherwise fashionable women to actually pay for dresses that make them look like colorblind Southern belles?"

He grinned. "Come on. It's not that bad."

"Easy for you to say. You don't have three very similar versions of that dress—in turquoise, pink and salmon—at home in your closet." She gave a tiny shudder.

His grin got a little broader. "Really? I'm a big fan of *Gone with the Wind*. You'll have to model them for me sometime."

She shook her head. "Not in this lifetime. I look like Little Bo-Peep after growth hormones."

He chuckled. "Okay...tell you what. How about if you just *pretend* to put them on? That'd be even better."

She started to tell him no way, then thought better of it. "What's in it for me?" she teased.

He appeared to consider, then leaned sideways and murmured, "How about if I pretend I'm Robert E. Lee and let you play with my sword?"

"Shane!" Laughing, she gave him a nudge to the shoulder. "That's awful." Yet even as she said it, she rejoiced in his playful attitude, finally admitting there had been a part of her that had feared this evening might turn out to be a painful reminder for him of his own marriage and subsequent loss.

Yet so far, the only awkward moments had come after the vows had been spoken, when they'd followed the wedding party out on to the church steps. While most of the attention had been on the bride and groom, it had soon become apparent to her that she and Shane were also a subject of some interest. Not only had there been lots of pointed glances, but a surprising number of people had made their way over to say hello and to mention, with varying degrees of diplomacy, how nice it was to see Shane out with someone. And though outwardly Shane had seemed calm and unruffled, Jessy had sensed his growing inner tension.

Now, after a trip through the reception line, a bite to eat, a glass of champagne and some gentle teasing, he appeared to be having a good time, however.

Jessy didn't kid herself. Not only was she glad for him, but she was also relieved for herself, since it was one more encouraging sign that their relationship was on solid footing. And that was important because she was finding it harder and harder not to tell him how much she loved him.

With an inner sigh, she acknowledged that when she'd initially decided to keep silent, she hadn't fully understood what she was getting into. It was only recently she'd come to see that every time she failed to say what was in her heart, she lost a little piece of herself.

Oddly enough, it was their confrontation about her evening at Margaret's last week that had opened her eyes. She'd suddenly seen that by doing what she thought Shane wanted, as opposed to following her own desires, she'd inadvertently hurt them both. And she'd suddenly known that she had to tell him the truth.

"You sure got awfully silent all of a sudden," Shane said, bringing her back to the present.

"I was just thinking how handsome you look," she said, gazing with open approval at his stylishly cut three-piece navy suit and the white shirt that showed off his olive skin and inky hair to perfection.

He shook his head. "If anybody looks good, it's you." He gazed admiringly over her fitted, pale blue silk suit, down the length of her nylon-sheathed legs and back up again. His gray eyes suddenly narrowed. "Those are panty hose, aren't they?"

She gave him her best sultry smile. "What do you think?"

Shane looked into her laughing eyes and felt an increasingly familiar combination of tenderness, affection, amusement and lust. "Damn it, Jessy. You're gonna be the death of me."

She smiled. "I'm working on it." Scooting closer, she deliberately pressed her silk covered knee against his leg as she reached over and rubbed her thumb against the corner of his mouth. "Frosting," she explained at his questioning look. She brought her thumb to her lips and sucked off the sweet white fleck, looking at him the entire while. "I can't take you anywhere."

In that instant, he felt as if they were the only two people in the world. And even though common sense warned that they were in a very public place, he couldn't refrain from capturing her hand and pressing a kiss to her fingertips.

"Hey, buddy," a jocular male voice said. "How you doing? I hope I'm not interrupting."

Shane swung around and found himself looking directly into the amused brown eyes of Kent Howard, an old high school friend. Letting loose of Jessy's hand, he took a firm grip on his composure. He came to his feet and offered a hand. "Kent. Nice to see you."

They shook briefly, then the other man waved him back in his seat, pulled up a chair and sat down himself, saying ruefully, "You may not think so in a minute. You see, your date here happens to be at the center of a wager." He turned his pleasant, slightly round face to Jessy. "Several of us decided you looked familiar, but my wife, Janie, and her friend over there—" he indicated a pair of women sitting with several other couples on the opposite side of the room "—swear it's because you teach at Wedgewood Elementary, where our son goes to school, while the rest of us are just as sure it's because you're a famous model."

"Ah." Jessy's smile was warm and amused.

"So what is it? Do I get to tell Janie she owes me a month of back rubs? Or—" he patted his slight beer belly "—do I have to face a month of aerobics?"

"Gosh." Her smile widened. "I hate to say it, but I hope you've got rhythm."

"Aagh!" He made a comically horrified face. "You're kidding! Really?"

Jessy laughed. "I'm afraid so. But I am flattered."

Amused despite himself, Shane made introductions. "Kent Howard, Jessy Ross."

"Ross?" An arrested expression came over the other man's face and he again looked intently at Jessy. "Not…Bailey's little sister?"

"One and the same."

"God, I remember you! You were just a skinny little kid!" He looked her up and down. "Hah! This is great. Wait until I tell Janie. She's not going to believe it. So, how's your brother?"

"He's fine."

"Is he still in Florida?"

They chatted for a few minutes, with Jessy bringing him up-to-date on Bailey's life, and then she said easily, "If you two gentlemen will excuse me, I think I'll make a run to the powder room." She stood. "It was nice to meet you again," she said to Kent. To Shane, she said, "I'll see *you* in a few minutes." With that, she strode away.

Both men watched her go. Kent gave a low whistle under his breath. "Wow. I can't believe that's really Bailey's beanpole kid sister. She turned into a stunner."

Shane tore his gaze away from Jessy's slender, graceful form. "Yeah, she did."

Kent shook his head. "Who'd have believed after all these years that the two of you would hook up?"

Shane said nothing since it wasn't the kind of question that required an answer.

Unperturbed, the other man continued cheerfully, "Then again, now that I think about it, I can remember how she used to look at you with those big blue eyes when we'd hang out at Bailey's. She was crazy about you then, and it's pretty obvious that hasn't changed. I guess sometimes puppy love really can turn into the real thing."

Shane stiffened. "What?"

Oblivious to the effect his words had had on Shane, Kent abruptly climbed to his feet, his gaze fixed on his own party. "I guess I need to go—Janie's giving me the high sign." He turned his attention to Shane one last time, his good-natured face benign. "It was great to see you, pal," he said sincerely. "Maybe the next time will be at your wedding, eh?" With a wink, he walked away.

Shane stared after him. Emotions cartwheeled through him—anger, amusement, denial, disbelief—as he replayed the other man's words.

Finally he shook his head as the ridiculousness of the exchange struck him. Jessy was in love with him? No way. Sure, they had incredible sexual chemistry, and an easy camaraderie thanks to their long-standing friendship. And yeah, he knew she cared about him. Hell, in his way he cared about her, too. But what they shared was a genuine fondness, a comfortable familiarity, and mutual, incendiary lust. It sure wasn't love.

"Hi, handsome."

As if conjured by his thoughts, he looked up to find her standing there, her hips subtly swaying as she kept time to the music coming from the dance floor. "Hi."

"Did your friend leave?"

"Yeah." He looked into her clear blue eyes, saw the warmth shining there, thought again about Kent's words, then shook them off. Plain and simple, the guy was mistaken. They were just…friends.

"Does that mean you're free to dance with me?"

He thought about holding her close, moving in time to the music. Okay, make that very good, very intimate friends.

"Shane?"

Still, why not? It beat the hell out of sitting here stewing about a lot of nonsense. "Sure."

Deliberately putting all speculation from his mind, he climbed to his feet. Resting his hand possessively on her back, he followed Jessy out onto the small dance floor.

Yet for all his denial, he couldn't help but notice how naturally they moved together.

Or how right it felt to hold her in his arms.

Jessy's faint moan of pleasure washed through the moonlit room. "Shane?"

"Hmm?"

"Is this as good for you as it is for me?"

"You want the truth?"

"Of course."

"Then sorry—I'm not that big on dairy products, Jess. When you brought up food, I was thinking a ham sandwich, not…Ben & Jerry's."

"Well, for heaven's sake, why didn't you say so?" In one lithe movement, she leaned sideways and snapped on the light above the stove. Setting aside her own quart of Jamaican toffee crunch, she reached over and plucked the offending carton from his hand.

"Hey," he protested, still clutching his spoon. "Isn't that a little extreme?"

She wagged her finger at him. "Nope. Rocky Road is too precious to squander on the unappreciative," she informed him, doing her best to look severe.

It was a wasted effort. Barely dressed in a brief black tank top and matching lace panties, with her hair tousled from his hands, her cheeks pink from his beard and her lips pouty and swollen from his mouth, she looked exactly like what she was—an incredibly sensual woman who had recently climbed out of his bed. "You don't say," he murmured.

She replaced the lid on the container and put it back in the freezer. "Oh, but I do." Opening the fridge, she began pulling out the makings for a sandwich and setting them on the counter. "Middle-of-the-night kitchen raids have certain rules."

"Like what?"

"Mmm, let's see. No guilt. No health food. And best of all—" she padded over to the bread drawer "—anything consumed after midnight is automatically calorie free."

"Ah. I see." With a murmured thanks, he accepted the napkin-wrapped sandwich she handed him. He took a bite. It was perfect, just the way he liked it. "So...did you have fun tonight?"

She picked up her ice cream, and sent him an arch look over the top of the container. "Which time?"

His mouth quirked. "I meant the wedding."

"Ah," she said blandly, nodding. "Of course. I told you. I love weddings." She paused for a moment, and when she spoke again, her tone had changed subtly. "What could be more wonderful than two people having enough faith to tie their lives together?"

She was serious, he realized with a sudden sense of uneasiness. "You believe in happily ever after? Even after what happened with your folks?" he said slowly, wondering what had possessed him to bring this up.

"Sure. I wouldn't wish what happened to them on anybody, but that doesn't mean there aren't some good marriages, too. Look at your parents. They're happy."

The exception to the rule. "Yeah, I suppose."

"I'm pretty sure it's all a matter of choosing the right person," she added thoughtfully.

Their gazes locked and all of a sudden Shane felt as if somebody had punched him hard in the stomach. As if a pair of blinders had been ripped off, he saw the look in her eyes—and he knew with a sickening certainty that he'd been deluding himself.

Kent Howard had been right. She *was* falling in love with him. And if just once in the past few weeks he'd looked beyond his own selfish needs and desires, or stopped to really think, he'd have known it, too. A sexual romp just wasn't in Jessy's nature; she had too much strength of character to give herself to him the way she had—unless she'd pledged her heart.

The irony was, even a relative stranger had been able to see it, he thought caustically. But not him. He'd been too blind, too self-absorbed, to see what was right in front of him. Just as he'd been with Marissa.

The old familiar self-disgust twisted through him. Hadn't he known better than to get involved with Jessy? Hadn't he known in his heart that she was too young, too idealistic, too naive and too trusting?

Damn straight he had. But he'd gone ahead anyway. If that wasn't proof that she deserved better, he didn't know what was.

"Shane?"

He glanced up. She was watching him, the beginning of worry creasing her brow. "Is something the matter?"

He hesitated. At the very least, he owed her the truth. Yet nobody knew better than he did that the truth could be brutal—and he hated the idea of hurting her, even a little.

Yeah? So why don't you be a man and let her down easy? Instead of dumping all over her, show her first what an insensitive bastard you can be. That way, when you finally do tell her it's over, she'll probably be relieved.

"Shane?"

"Everything's fine," he said abruptly. "I guess I'm not very hungry after all," he improvised, turning away from her too-knowing gaze and setting his half-eaten sandwich in the sink. "I'm sorry you went to all that trouble."

"No problem," she said quickly. "But...are you sure you're okay? You looked sort of strange there for a second. Like you'd lost your best friend."

In a way, he supposed he had—she just didn't know it yet. "I'm fine. It's just...there's something I need to talk to you about."

"Really?" An odd expression, almost like anticipation, flickered across her face. "Well good, because there's something I want to talk to you about, too." She set the container of ice cream aside and nodded encouragingly. "You first."

"All right." He took a ruthless hold on his seesawing emotions and tried to sound nonchalant. "I think we need to cool things for a while."

She stared at him blankly. "What?"

"You have to admit—" he shoved away from the counter, afraid he'd be tempted to touch her if he didn't put some distance between them "—we've been spending an awful lot of time together. It's been fun, but I think we could both use a breather."

"But—"

"It's nothing personal, Jess," he said briskly. "I just need a little space."

She took a deep breath. "Is it…is it Marissa, Shane? Are you still in love with her?"

"Hell, no," he said emphatically before he could catch himself. Yet he couldn't stand the thought of Jessy comparing herself to his late wife—and thinking she'd come out short. "Things are just getting a little intense, that's all."

"I…see." Her movements jerky, she began putting things away.

"It's not a problem, is it? I mean, we did have an agreement—right?"

She was silent. Yet after a moment her inherent honesty kicked in. Reluctantly she nodded. "Yes, we did."

"Okay." With calculated callousness, he pretended to yawn. "Now that that's settled, what did you want to tell me?"

She shook her head. "It was nothing. Not really."

"You sure?"

"Yes." She lifted her head and for the first time he saw the full extent of the hurt glittering in her eyes. Damning himself a thousand times, he nevertheless yawned again. "Then if we're done, I think I'll turn in. I've got a full day tomorrow. You don't mind, do you?"

"No. You go ahead."

"Good night, then." He forced himself to walk away, telling himself over and over that he'd done the right thing. That it might be hard now, but it was still a hell of a lot better than if he'd let things go on the way he had.

So why, he wondered, as he walked slowly into his dark, empty bedroom, did it feel so bad?

Eleven

"**D**o again?" Chloe asked.

Jessy started to say no, then stopped as she looked down into the toddler's pleading face.

"Pweese?" The child's big blue eyes gleamed with hope.

She sighed. "Okay. But this is *it*," she said firmly, reopening the picture book on her lap for the fourth time that morning. "What's that?" she asked, pointing at a now very familiar picture.

"A blue doggy!" Chloe said happily, scooting a little closer on the big black-and-white couch.

"And this one?" Jessy indicated another brightly colored drawing.

"A gween cat!"

"Right again."

The toddler beamed and flipped the page. Before Jessy could ask, she recited, "A black bird." She turned the page again. "A wed goadpish." And then, pressing her finger to the picture of a rabbit the color of lemons, "An oh-low bunny. Pweety!"

"Yes, it is," Jessy agreed. One by one, they went through the remaining page, making note of the purple cow, the orange pig and a variety of other creatively colored creatures, until Jessy once more flipped to the front so they could start the second half of their reading ritual. "Okay, now we'll see how high you can count."

"Okeydokey."

She opened to the first page.

"One..." This time Chloe waited for her to turn the pages. "Two...twee...nine—seben!" she finished with a giggle.

Jessy gave her a heartfelt hug. "That's great! You got one, two and three right! That's really good, sweetheart. But then it's *four* and *five,* remember?"

The toddler's brow crinkled, and then she nodded emphatically. "One, two, twee...four, fibe!"

Ignoring the faint din as a buzzer sounded from the other room, Jessy gave her another hug. "Wow. That's perfect! You're so smart!"

The little girl beamed and began to bounce up and down. "Do again? Pweese?"

Amused, Jessy shook her head. "No way, kiddo. A deal's a deal. Now let me up so I can go get the clothes from the dryer."

Chloe managed to look crestfallen for all of a second before her chin came up and she said brightly, "I help!" Clambering off the couch, she dashed for the utility room.

Jessy shook her head, following fondly after the child. One thing about Chloe, she could be counted on to let you know exactly what she felt.

It was just too bad the same couldn't be said for Shane.

As simply as that, the good mood Jessy had been struggling to maintain since climbing out of bed that morning slid away. Although she managed to keep up a front for Chloe as they transferred the dry clothes into the laundry basket and carried it back out to the couch, she was relieved when the little girl decided she'd really rather play with her blocks than fold clothes.

Jessy picked up a small shirt and went to work. Outside, the sun glowed warm and golden. The sky was blue, the air was clear and the surface of the lake was as smooth as a mirror. It was going to be another perfect summer day.

Or it would be, Jessy corrected, as she smoothed the wrinkles out of a pint-size pair of overalls...if not for Shane.

The second she realized what she'd just thought, she gave a silent scream of frustration. Why couldn't she quit thinking about him? After all, it had been ten days since he'd announced he needed a "little" space. Since then, she'd barely seen him, thanks to his suddenly pressing schedule. There had been lots of late nights, dawn departures and missed dinners. There had also been a flurry of overnight business trips, including the one that had stretched to include the past weekend.

Jessy pursed her lips. About the only positive notes were that she now knew that she'd been right, and that whatever the problem was, it wasn't that he was still pining for his late wife. And that when Shane had deigned to be home during the daylight hours, he'd spent his time with Chloe. And though Jessy suspected part of the reason was so he wouldn't wind up alone with *her*, she was still glad. At least something positive had come out of this mess.

Not that she blamed everything on Shane. She realized now that she'd made a huge mistake that night in the kitchen. She should have asked flat out what was going on. She should have demanded to know why he suddenly felt things were too intense. And she should have insisted he tell her exactly what he meant by taking a "breather."

In her own defense, at the time she'd been so stunned by what he was saying that it hadn't seemed quite real. There she'd been, still warm and tingling from his lovemaking, looking for the right time to tell him she loved him—and *poof!* It was over.

It had just taken her a while to realize it.

And ever since she had, she'd been on an emotional roller coaster, she acknowledged as she shifted the last of the laundry into the basket, sank down on the couch and let her head fall back against the cushion. First, she'd been hurt and bewildered. Then she'd tried to objectively analyze the situation. When that hadn't worked—thanks to a lack of basic information—she'd told herself to have some faith, that maybe if she just gave Shane some space, he'd come around. When the days passed and it became obvious that wasn't going to happen, she'd gotten angry and tried to tell herself she didn't give a damn about him.

Unfortunately she'd never been a very good liar and was particularly bad at deceiving herself. So, while her anger had felt kind of liberating and had sustained her for several days, deep down she'd known she still cared. Enough that she'd finally swallowed her pride, gotten up extra early yesterday morning and told Shane they needed to talk. To which he'd replied, "Later," and walked purposefully out the door.

Well, it had been more than twenty-four hours and so far *later* hadn't come. And she was starting to believe it was never going to—not if Shane had his way.

So why the heck should he? she wondered suddenly, sitting up. After all, she'd tried to accommodate his feelings—and this was what it had gotten her. Hadn't she learned anything from what had happened eight years ago? She'd kept her feelings to herself then, and he'd married someone else. It was doubtful a declaration of love would have changed anything, but she'd never know for certain.

Was she going to do the same thing again? Remain silent? Pretend she didn't care? Go away quietly?

No. While it was true she couldn't force him to talk to her, it was also true she wasn't a prisoner in this house. There was no reason she had to sit here and meekly wait for him to make a move. She could make a few moves of her own. And if he really wanted to end things, then he could just have the decency to say so.

But not until she reminded him exactly what he was giving up.

She sat still a moment, considering what she ought to do for an opening salvo. Then she sat up a little straighter, reached over, picked up the cordless phone and punched in the number for his office.

He'd wanted a breather? Well, he'd had one.

As of now, it was over.

"You're sure you don't want me to tell him you're here?" Shane's secretary asked, his hand on the outer door.

Jessy smiled reassuringly. "Positive. I appreciate you

sticking around to let me in, Jeffrey, but I'll take it from here. Like I told you on the phone, I want to surprise him.''

''Yeah,'' he said thoughtfully, eyeing the picnic basket she'd hauled in and set by the inner door. ''I guess he could use a break. Things are really slow, what with everyone being on vacation this time of year. All of his appointments keep canceling and I think he's been sort of frustrated lately.''

She digested that rather interesting piece of information. ''Really?''

''Yeah.'' He bit his lip as if he'd like to say more, then seemed to remember who signed his paychecks. He pushed open the door. ''I hope you have fun.''

''We will.'' She smiled goodbye, waited for the door to close behind him, then glanced at Chloe, who was riding her hip. ''Whether Daddy likes it or not—right, sweetie?''

The toddler nodded agreeably. ''Wight!''

Jessy gave the child an affectionate look. ''Too bad Daddy isn't more like you,'' she murmured. Taking a deep breath to steady her nerves, she squared her shoulders. Then she walked resolutely to Shane's office door, eased it open and peeked inside.

Although it was still sunny outside, the room was dusky with shadows, courtesy of the north-facing windows. For a second she was discomfited to hear voices. Had she misunderstood Jeffrey when he'd said Shane was alone? Then she realized the sound came from a portable television set in an opened cabinet across from the couch at the far end of the room. A quick glance at the screen revealed that it was tuned to a baseball game.

Not that Shane was watching it. On the contrary, he stood at the window, gazing out. To her surprise, instead of his usual well-kept appearance, his tie was askew, his sleeves rolled back, his hair mussed, his shoulders slumped.

He looked very much alone. And more than a little dejected.

Jessy pursed her lips and told herself sternly she absolutely, positively, was not going to feel any sympathy for him. Not after the way he'd walked away from her without any real explanation. Not after he'd tried to fob her off with "later."

Lifting her chin, she gave the door a nudge, hiked Chloe up a little higher and raised her voice to be heard over the TV announcer. "Knock, knock."

Shane whipped around so fast it was a miracle he didn't hurt himself. "Jess?" For a moment he actually looked glad to see her.

"Hi. Can we come in?"

"Yeah, I guess. What are you doing here?"

Bending down, she gripped the handle of the picnic basket, straightened and started across the low-pile carpet. "We decided that since you couldn't get home for dinner because you had so much work to do, we'd bring dinner to you."

She raised the heavy basket and plunked it down on the pristine surface of his desk. It was bereft of so much as a single piece of paper, she noted with interest. That prompted her to take a quick look around, from the darkened computer screen, to the bare gleaming surface of the conference table, to the dent in the navy couch cushions that suggested someone had been lying there quite recently. For a guy who was supposedly overburdened with work, Shane was doing a darn good job of hiding it.

She looked over at him.

He had the grace to appear sheepish for an instant. A second later his expression hardened, however, as if he'd decided the best defense was a good offense. "How'd you get in here, anyway? I thought everyone had left. Wasn't the door locked?"

"We were lucky enough to catch Jeffrey as he was leaving," she said airily, strolling toward him. She glanced at Chloe. "Weren't we, sweetie?"

Chloe nodded, the perfect pint-size accomplice. "Jeffie go bye-bye." She stretched her arms toward her father as they got closer. "Want Dada."

"Of course you do," Jessy murmured, feeling a jolt of satisfaction as Shane's gaze skimmed the length of her bare legs and a dull red flush tinged his cheeks. She'd deliberately chosen the short, clingy, black T-shirt dress and strappy sandals for exactly that reaction. She stopped a foot away from him and leaned forward to make the transfer. "I guess she got spoiled by having you around so much," she told him.

Their gazes meshed. He was the first to look away. "I've been busy," he said gruffly, reaching forward. "I've been doing the best I can."

"Of course you have," she said gently. Looking into his dark gray eyes, she deliberately relaxed the arm she had under Chloe.

"Careful!" Shane made a grab for the child and easily caught her—but not before Jessy's surprise move caused his hand to slide the length of her bare arm and brush the softness of her breast.

"Sorry," she said innocently. She watched with secret satisfaction as his mouth tightened and he took an abrupt step back. "I don't know what happened. For a moment there, I just felt...weak."

His eyes came up and narrowed on her face. "Jess—"

"Chloe and I cooked all afternoon so we could surprise you, didn't we, sweetie?"

The child nodded.

"We made fried chicken and potato salad. And we brought French bread and strawberries and double fudge brownies for dessert."

"I hepped," Chloe told her father.

Shane tore his gaze away from Jessy and looked down at the little girl. "You did, huh?"

She nodded. "Uh-huh. And I eated one, two, twee...four, fibe!" She proudly held up the fingers of one hand.

He looked surprised. "Hey, that's really good."

Again she nodded. "I'm smart."

"Yeah." His face softened and he gave her an awkward hug. "You are."

To her annoyance, Jessy felt her heart turn to mush. Determined to regain her composure, she walked over to the basket, opened the top and pulled out a red-and-white checked tablecloth. "So what do you think?" she said, looking around again. "Shall I set the food out on the coffee table? That way we can sit on the floor like a real picnic."

"Jess," Shane remonstrated.

She glanced over at him. "You do like fried chicken, don't you?"

"Well, yeah, but—"

"And you haven't eaten already, have you?"

"Well, no, but—"

"I brought a cloth to protect the carpeting from Chloe."

"That's good, but—"

"So what's the problem?"

"The problem," he said flatly, "is you and me, here, like this."

"Shane," she said reproachfully. "Relax. What's one little family dinner between friends?" She paused, then gave him her best uncertain look. "I mean, we are still friends—aren't we?"

"Well, yeah, but—"

"Then relax. Really. All we're going to do is eat and talk. You can tell me about all these trips you've been taking. And I'll tell you about this wonderful little house I've found to rent." She reached out, grasped his hand and gave it a gentle squeeze. "Trust me. It'll be fun."

The sound of muffled laughter drifted from the outer office.

Frowning, Shane told himself to ignore it and tried to concentrate instead on the marketing projection laid out on his desk.

Overall, things looked good, he concluded. As long as they continued to put out a quality product, were careful not to expand too quickly and saturate the market, there seemed to be no reason why TopLine couldn't enjoy steady growth for the next five years. Although, judging from the most recent figures, in order to accomplish that he was going to have to think about hiring another salesman—

A light, distracting chuckle wafted from the other room, disrupting his train of thought.

He fought a wave of irritation and glanced at his watch. It read twelve-fifteen, and his annoyance dissipated somewhat at the knowledge that whoever was goofing off was presumably doing it on their lunch hour.

He went back to the report. Yet when the laughter erupted again and he realized a few seconds later that

he'd just read an entire page without a lick of compre-
hension, he threw up his hands. Exasperated by his in-
ability to focus, he shoved back his chair and paced restlessly across the room, asking himself what the problem
was.

*Oh, yeah, right. Like it's some big secret? Don't kid
yourself, Wyatt. You know exactly what's bothering you
and it's not a few chuckles coming from the other room.
It's this whole thing with Jessy, and you know it.*

With a groan of frustration, he flung himself down on
the couch and let his head fall back, staring blankly up
at the ceiling.

Up until the day before yesterday, while he hadn't
been exactly happy, at least he'd been able to maintain.
By keeping busy and severely limiting his time alone
with her, he'd been able to pretend that the past six
weeks hadn't happened, that he was still the same person
he'd been before she'd moved in and they'd become
intimate.

And then she'd shown up with that damned little im-
promptu picnic, and then dropped by again yesterday
morning to see if he wanted to go out for coffee, and
suddenly he hadn't been so okay anymore. With just
those two encounters, she'd managed to stir up a jumble
of feelings he was finding impossible to ignore.

There was lust, for starters. It, at least, was straight-
forward and understandable, since a guy would have to
be unconscious not to notice the way she'd looked in
that stretchy black dress or react to all those friendly
little touches she'd unthinkingly bestowed on him. In
much the same way, he would have to have been dead
yesterday not to respond when she'd stumbled on her
way to the door and fallen against him, pressing all her
soft, familiar curves against him. Given the vigorous

way his body had already been protesting his return to celibacy, both encounters had been similar to pouring gasoline on his dangerously smoldering libido. Each time they'd said goodbye, every muscle he possessed had quivered with the effort it took not to toss her down on the nearest horizontal surface and show her just how glad a certain part of him was to see her.

So it was no big surprise that he was also feeling massively frustrated.

What was a surprise, however, was that his frustration wasn't entirely sexual. On the contrary, a large portion of it stemmed from the alarming knowledge that he'd really, really enjoyed being with her. Just for the company. With both of them fully clothed.

Because, as promised, the picnic *had* been fun. He'd tried his best not to enjoy it, but the food had been delicious, Chloe had been delightful and Jessy had been utterly disarming. She'd told him all about the house she'd found to rent. She'd explained why she usually preferred living alone to sharing, her eyes dancing as she recounted her experiences with a woman she'd laughingly called the roommate from hell. She'd talked about her most memorable students, some pretty interesting parents and the trials and tribulations of dealing with a district administration that sometimes seemed to care more about the bottom line than the students. She'd been warm and charming, entertaining and undemanding, she'd smelled fantastic and looked even better.

At some point he'd begun to wish the evening wouldn't end.

Similarly, although he'd said no to coffee yesterday, even going so far as to take her to task for interrupting him, a part of him had hated to see her go, while another part had wanted to go with her.

And that, of course, was the problem. Because nothing had changed—he still wasn't the right man for her. She could do better. She deserved someone without all his baggage, someone who could offer her an untroubled future, someone who could love her the way she deserved.

Not that she'd seemed exactly devastated by the recent turn of events, he thought irritably, his focus returning to the night before. While he'd stayed away from his own home, given up great sex and spent more nights than he cared to count lying awake worrying about her, *she* hadn't seemed terribly affected one way or another.

Yeah? So? Isn't that what you wanted? If you had an ounce of class, you'd be happy for her. Instead, here you sit, selfishly thinking it wouldn't kill her to pine for you just a little bit.

Another burst of laughter, this one louder than the rest, sounded from the outer office. Suddenly out of patience, he climbed to his feet, strode over to the door and flung it open. "I hate to interrupt," he began sarcastically, "but some of us are trying to work—" He broke off in disbelief.

"Hi!" Jessy sat perched on the corner of Jeffrey's desk, dressed in a sleeveless yellow blouse that showed off her tan and a brief, flowered skirt that, just like the dress last night, exposed way too much of her legs.

He could feel a muscle quiver in his jaw. "What are you doing here?"

"I stopped by to show you some photos I took of Chloe," she said cheerfully, indicating the glossy prints spread out on the desk. "But Jeffrey said you were going over some reports and didn't want to be disturbed so—"

"I'm finished," he said flatly.

"Okay. Great." She uncrossed her legs and slid off

the desk, her skirt riding dangerously high before her feet touched the ground. "I'll be there in a minute, okay?" With a dismissive smile, she turned her back and resumed her discussion with Jeffrey, her shoulder touching his as she leaned over, picked up one of the photos and said, "Now, this is one of my personal favorites…"

Shane felt a sharp pain radiate through his face and realized he was grinding his teeth.

So much for pining away…

Suddenly furious and not sure why, he turned on his heel and strode back into his office.

Shane awoke Friday morning with a crick in his neck. He lay where he was for a moment, then gradually realized that something was wrong. Not only did his pillow feel firmer than usual, but the bed didn't feel right, either.

He opened his eyes and got a momentary shock as he realized he was lying on the couch in his office, with his head propped on a loose cushion. It was another few moments, however, before he came fully awake and realized what had happened.

By the time Jessy had left yesterday, he'd been totally bent out of shape. He'd had no time to dwell on it, however, as there had been a sudden flurry of minor crises that had all required his attention. When things finally had calmed down, it had been well after seven. Very much aware that he was in no mood to face Jess, he'd called home and left a message on the machine telling her not to expect him anytime soon. Then he'd ordered a pizza and turned on the TV. He remembered eating, and tuning into the Mariners/Yankees game, and then…nothing.

Apparently the stress of the past few days, as well as a general lack of sleep, had finally caught up with him.

Sitting up, he realized something else. Sometime in the past dozen hours, he'd come to a decision. He was going to tell Jessy it was over. Furthermore, as much as he'd like to think otherwise, there was no use telling himself that he was doing it for her benefit. Straight out, his control was wearing thin and he wasn't sure how much longer he could trust himself around her. If he didn't end things now, he wasn't sure he could.

He'd tell her tonight. That is, unless she showed up at the office first, he thought ruefully. Where didn't matter. Whenever and wherever it happened, the important thing was to get the issue resolved so they were both free to get on with their lives.

The decision made, he sat there for a moment, waiting to feel some relief. Instead, all he felt was numb—except for an inexplicable melancholy that seemed to press on him like a weight.

He climbed slowly to his feet. Grabbing the change of clothes he kept in the office, he set out for the employee gym to shave and shower.

Incredibly, despite a pain in his belly that made him wonder if he was getting an ulcer, the day flew by. It wasn't until well after four that he got a chance to call home. There was no answer, so he wasn't surprised when there was a soft knock at the door a short while later.

"Who is it?" he asked, even though he was pretty sure he already knew. The pain in his stomach got a little bigger.

To his surprise, it wasn't Jessy who stuck her head inside, however. It was Jeffrey. "I'm leaving for the night, Mr. Wyatt," the young man said, a worried look

on his face. "But I just found this on the floor under my
desk—" he crossed over and handed Shane a memo slip
"—and I think you'd better read it. Dora must have
taken it ~~when~~ she covered for me at lunch and somehow
it got misplaced. I'm really sorry."

Shane gave the piece of paper a quick glance, then set
it down and looked up at the other man. "That's all
right, Jeffrey," he said brusquely. "I'll take care of it.
Have a nice weekend."

"You, too."

"Oh, yeah."

The minute he was gone, Shane picked up the note
again. It read:

Mr. Wyatt—
   Jessica Ross called to let you know she's been
invited to a friend's for the weekend. She says she
will plan on taking Chloe with her unless she hears
from you otherwise and will be leaving around
three o'clock. She says if she doesn't talk to you,
to tell you to have a nice weekend.
Dora

Shane stared at the paper in disbelief. Well, damn.
There went that plan.

What the hell did he do now?

Twelve

Jessy wasn't sure what kind of reception she expected when she got home from her friend Marci's cabin.

At best, she hoped Shane would have come to his senses and decided he couldn't live without her.

At worst, she was afraid he wouldn't even be there, but would have gone off instead on another business trip.

What she didn't expect was for him to be waiting for her at the door, as stiff as a treated two-by-four, wearing his oldest blue jeans, a gray T-shirt and an expression as black as a thunderstorm.

"Hi," she said, hiding her sudden uncertainty under a bright smile as he held the door for her and she entered the house. "How was your weekend?"

He flicked shut the door. Ignoring her question, he gave her a quick once-over, his eyes narrowing as he saw she was wearing yet another dress, this one a casual tank style in soft blue. He didn't comment, however.

Instead, he focused his attention on Chloe, who was snoring quietly in her arms. "How long has she been asleep?"

"About twenty minutes."

He gave a snort of disgust. "Her bedtime was an hour ago. Give her to me and I'll put her in bed where she belongs."

She gave him a long look. He didn't blink, just stared intractably back. "Okay," she said evenly. She transferred the baby to him, feeling a mixture of love and exasperation as he marched off without another word. Shaking her head, she headed out to the car to get her things, telling herself to look on the bright side.

At least he was here.

That was good, because she'd had lots of time to think the past two days. And it hadn't taken her long to decide that while she'd had her fun last week, the time had come to act like a grown-up. She and Shane needed to talk, whether he liked it or not.

She was just starting down the hall to her room when he came out of Chloe's. He shut the door and stalked in her direction. "I'd like to speak to you," he said tightly as he passed her. "In the family room."

Then again, maybe that talk could wait until morning, she thought, belatedly remembering the old warning to be careful what you wish for. "All right." Feeling a trifle apprehensive, she set down her and Chloe's bags, took a deep breath, reversed direction and followed after him, only to come to a sudden stop as she crossed the threshold.

She looked around in disbelief. The place was a mess. In the kitchen, newspapers, some half-eaten frozen dinners and a handful of empty beer bottles littered the counters, sharing space with a trail of spilled coffee grounds, a trio of open cereal boxes and, inexplicably, two quart cans of motor oil.

In the family room itself, a makeshift bed had been made on the couch, while a pizza box, some half-empty glasses and a stack of soiled plates covered the end table. Next to the VCR, a half-dozen video rentals were strewn over the floor, and there was a stain on the rug that hadn't been there before.

Shane had obviously been home all weekend, Jessy realized. Yet he was normally so neat... She looked around again, wondering what, if anything, such disarray meant.

"Where were you?" he said abruptly.

The curt question brought her attention back to the matter at hand. She looked over at him. He was standing at the sliding glass doors with his back to her, his tension obvious in the rigid line of his back.

"A friend of mine has a cabin on Vashon Island." She walked over and joined him at the window. Beyond the glass, long slivers of silver light slanted across the lake, a last show of beauty before the sun set for the night.

He didn't acknowledge her presence. Instead he shoved his hands into his pockets and continued to stare woodenly out. "Does this friend have a phone?"

"As a matter of fact, no, she doesn't."

He was silent. Yet she would have sworn there was a slight lessening of his tension—until he suddenly turned without warning and said furiously, "What the hell did you think you were doing, taking off like that without even talking to me?"

She stared at him in astonishment. "*Excuse* me?"

"You heard me. Answer the damn question!"

"Didn't you get my message?"

"Yeah, I got your message—for all the good it did me! You should have waited to talk to me before you left."

She felt her own temper start to ignite. "Oh, right! For your information, I'd planned to talk to you Thursday night. Only you never bothered to come home—remember?"

"I left a message," he said curtly.

"Yeah? Well, so did I. Only unlike you, I didn't have another option, since the woman answering the phone at your office made it very clear you'd left instructions you weren't to be disturbed. It's certainly not my fault you never called me back."

"Hell, by the time I found out what was going on, you were already gone."

"So? Welcome to my world!"

"What does that mean?"

"It means, get real, Shane. At least I tried. I don't recall you checking in with me about *anything* lately."

His jaw tightened obstinately. "This is different."

"Oh, yeah? Why?"

"You took my daughter—"

"Oh, please. Don't you dare use Chloe as an excuse. This has nothing to do with her, and you know it. You just don't like being on the receiving end when it comes to not having control."

"You don't know what you're talking about!"

"The heck I don't!" She took a deep breath and tried to rein in her temper. "Although, I will agree that I don't think that's the real issue here."

He glared at her, refusing to give an inch. "Oh, really? And just what do you think is?"

"I think you had a long, lonely weekend—"

"Oh, for God's sake—!" he uttered in disgust.

"And what's more, I think you missed me and are just too damn stubborn to admit it!" For the life of her, she didn't realize that was what she'd intended to say until she heard the words come out of her mouth. Yet she knew in her heart she was right. And the way he suddenly stiffened told her she'd struck a nerve.

As did the suddenly shuttered look on his face. "You're wrong," he said flatly.

"Really? Prove it."

He made a rude, dismissive sound, but his eyes were suddenly wary. "How?"

"Tell me you don't want this as much as I do." Before he could divine her intention, or she could lose her nerve, she grabbed a fistful of his shirt, yanked him toward her and kissed him for all she was worth.

For one terrible moment, his entire body went rigid, and she thought she'd completely misread the situation. Then a tremor went through him and, with a sound that was close to a growl, he wrapped his arms around her and pulled her close, holding onto her for all he was worth.

The relief was overwhelming. So was the warm, solid feeling of him against her.

"Oh, Shane." Coming up for air, she buried her face in his neck, breathing in his clean, male scent.

He nuzzled her hair. "You're right. I missed you so much." His voice was raw.

"Shh, it's all right, I missed you, too."

"This place was like a morgue without you."

Clinging together and exchanging feverish kisses, they made their way to the couch. Refusing to let her go, Shane kept his arm around her waist as he leaned over and shoved a pillow and blanket out of the way. He urged her to lie down.

Jessy had other ideas. "No, wait." To his obvious surprise, she undid the catch at the top of his jeans and lowered his zipper, then pushed down his briefs, closing her hand around him as he sprang free of the constricting fabric.

"Jess—"

"It's all right," she murmured, leaning forward and kissing him. He felt hard and hot and satiny smooth in her hand. With a firm grip, she measured him with her fist, needing to touch him.

"Jess!" he protested again, this time with a strangled groan. "Stop—unless you want this to end right now."

She reluctantly let go of him, and it was her turn to gasp as he promptly sank onto the couch, reached under her dress and stripped off her panties, then pulled her down so she straddled his lap.

"Yes," he said forcefully as she lowered herself onto him, his eyes glinting when she bit her lip as her body adjusted to his fullness. "You feel so good."

"Oh, Shane, so do you. It's been too long." Thrusting her hands into his hair, she pressed her mouth to his and slowly began to move.

"Oh, yeah," he said raggedly between kisses. "Like that. That's perfect." His hands found her breasts, shaping them through the thin cotton knit. He rubbed them with his palms, then pressed them together and gently squeezed her aching nipples between his index fingers and his thumbs. "Like you."

She moaned and arched her back and her head fell back. "Oh, yes…"

"You've got the most beautiful breasts," he whispered, trailing his lips down her throat. He squeezed his fingers together again, careful to apply just the right amount of pressure.

Whimpering, Jessy rocked against him a little faster, took him a little deeper, feeling the familiar anticipation as her body began to ride a crest of pleasure. Even so, she was totally unprepared when Shane suddenly grabbed her hips and pressed her down at the same second that he braced his feet on the floor and surged upright.

Sensation rocketed through her. She felt him, a hot, solid strength inside and out. Her inner muscles tightened, squeezing around him. And then that wave rolled over her and she opened her eyes and everything she felt for him came pouring out. "I love you," she said fiercely, staring into his passion-dark eyes. "I love you."

Shane gazed back, his throat going tight as he realized how desperately he'd needed to hear her say those words. A fierce sense of possessiveness swept over him, a primal need to brand her as his own. He began to thrust harder and faster, gritting his teeth as he felt his climax approach. And then his hips jerked and his body arched and for an indeterminate time he couldn't think, he could only feel—the sweetness of Jessy's mouth; the pounding of his heart; his voice crying her name; the pleasure flooding through him.

When the last spasm ended, he felt as limp as a baby. Closing his eyes, he let his head fall back against the top of the couch and sat there, spent.

It was a while before he stirred. Opening his eyes, he looked down and saw Jessy's golden brown head nestled trustingly against him. Tenderness curled through him, as warm and potent as a shot of whiskey.

It was no use kidding himself, he realized, finally facing the knowledge he'd been struggling against all weekend. He loved her. More than was probably wise. Certainly more than was safe. Definitely more than he could deny.

Not that he hadn't tried. With a rueful smile, he acknowledged that he'd spent the whole weekend doing just that. Like a beast in a cave, he'd hunkered down and tried hard not to think. Instead he'd wrapped himself in a cloak of anger as he'd made a last-ditch effort to deny what he really felt.

But then, he was good at that. After he'd found out about Marissa's betrayal, he'd managed to shut out the world. He'd embraced his isolation, he'd guarded his independence, he'd even accepted celibacy—whatever it took to remain emotionally indifferent.

And then Jessy had shown up and began chipping away at the barriers he'd thrown up. Bit by bit, she'd whittled away at him with her warmth and her laughter, until, no matter how he tried to convince himself otherwise, he'd felt himself reconnecting with the world.

Until the night of the wedding, when he'd panicked. Not, as he'd told himself then, because it had finally dawned on him that she loved him. But because on some level he'd realized that he loved her and it had scared the hell out of him. Which wasn't surprising, since he knew from bitter experience how much love could hurt.

Even so, these past two weeks without her had been sheer hell. He'd missed her scent and the sound of her voice. He'd missed coming home to her at night and waking up with her in the morning. He'd missed her joy, her laughter and her positive outlook on life. He'd missed her strength, her integrity, her loving.

He'd missed her.

And he knew that, scared or not, he had to tell her the truth. She had a right to know—everything. Even if it meant the worst happened and she quit loving him.

He had to take the chance. Because, as he knew too well, without trust, love was nothing.

He smoothed her hair, his mouth twisting ironically as he saw that his hand was shaking. "Jess?"

"Hmm?"

"We need to talk."

She must have heard the strain in his voice because she opened her eyes and sat up, her look of contentment fading at what she saw in his face. "All right. But if it's about what I said, I meant it and I'm not going to take it back. I love you, Shane."

He shook his head. "Don't. Please. Not until you hear what I have to say."

Her gaze troubled, she gave him a long searching look, then nodded and stood. He climbed to his feet as well. Straightening his clothes, he tried to decide where to start. Yet deep down he knew that nothing less than the whole story would do.

Outside, dusk was giving way to night and the first stars were beginning to appear in the sky. He reached over, switched on the lamp, took a deep breath and simply began, since he didn't know what else to do.

"When Marissa and I got married, I thought it was going to be the way it was with my parents. I thought we'd be lovers, best friends, equal partners. And, pretty arrogantly, I thought it would be easy.

"It wasn't. It was hard, and that caught me off guard. So did the discovery that the qualities I'd found so attractive in Marissa while we were dating—her dependence, her possessiveness, the way she expected me to make all the decisions—were rapidly losing their charm. She was the same person she'd always been, and it doesn't say very much about me that the more demanding she became, the more I retreated.

"The year before Chloe was born was the worst." He paced across the room, dreading what came next. Jess had always looked at him through such rose-colored glasses; he hated having to admit what a fool he'd been. But it couldn't be avoided. He stopped and faced her. "Things had really taken off with TopLine, and I was doing a lot of traveling. Marissa resented that, and the business, and anything else that claimed my attention, and it seemed like whenever we were together she was either angry or in tears. And then, just when I started to think we weren't going to make it, everything suddenly got better. Almost overnight, Marissa seemed to grow up and accept that I couldn't be there for her every single minute. I was so glad, it didn't occur to me to question it."

He raked a hand through his hair, surprised at the absence of his usual grinding self-disgust, until it dawned on him that it almost felt as if he were talking about someone else. "Even though I was still gone a lot, we had several peaceful, happy months, and when she told me she was pregnant, I was thrilled. Finally everything seemed to be falling into place. When Chloe was born, it was the happiest day of my life. Finally we were a real family.

"Then there was the accident." He shook his head, remembering. "I couldn't believe it. It seemed so cruel that just when things were beginning to work, it was over. Yet as hard as it was, I knew I had to get through it for Chloe's sake. And I was doing all right—*we* were doing all right—until the week before her first birthday."

Jessy could feel her pulse start to race. She remembered how oddly he'd behaved at Chloe's birthday party and realized she was finally going to learn what had happened that had changed him so much. Yet even so, she wasn't prepared for what came next.

"Chloe caught a cold. It wasn't much, just the sniffles. But after losing Marissa, I panicked and took her to the pediatrician's. The nurse did the usual stuff, then left us alone in the examining room to wait for the doctor. Maybe it was because Marissa had always been the one who'd taken Chloe for her checkups, or maybe I was just curious, but I picked up the chart and leafed through it. There wasn't much to it since Chloe was so young— just a graph tracking her height and weight, a record of her inoculations, the doctor's notes and an exam chart, with her date of birth, the name of the hospital where she'd been delivered, that sort of stuff. Most of it was information I'd already seen—except for her blood type. The chart read Type *A*. I knew that was a mistake because Marissa and I were both Type *O*, which meant our child had to be *O*, as well."

Jessy felt the blood drain from her face as she realized what he was saying.

"When the doctor came in, I went ballistic, demanding to know how they could make such a dangerous mistake. What kind of incompetents were they? What if something happened and my daughter needed a transfusion? And the whole time I was yelling, my heart was breaking. But I wouldn't admit it—not even when it was confirmed that Chloe really was Type *A*. I kept thinking it was a mistake right up until the results came back from the DNA test."

"Oh, Shane." Unable to stand the anguish in his voice, she crossed the space between them and laid her hand on his shoulder. "I'm so sorry. How terrible for you."

He stepped back, out of reach, turning away to stare

into the gathering darkness. With a sense of shock she realized that he wasn't done, although she couldn't imagine anything more heartbreaking than what she'd just heard. Yet it was clear from his rigid posture that he considered what was coming to be even worse.

"You're right. It was terrible. For a while, I wasn't sure I was going to make it. But I did. I survived. Only there was a price. Because even though I knew in my head that Chloe wasn't responsible for her mother's actions, at first whenever I looked at her I'd think about Marissa's betrayal. And then, even though I still loved her, I found myself keeping her at arm's length, withholding a part of myself, unable to get past my own screwed-up feelings. And the longer I put off dealing with it, the worse it seemed to get." He took a shuddering breath and forced himself to meet her gaze directly. "Now you tell me, Jess—what kind of man treats an innocent baby that way?"

His eyes were anguished and the corners of his mouth—that sensual, wonderful mouth that had kissed her so passionately just minutes ago—were pinched. Jessy swallowed as everything fell into place and she realized that, as shocking as the secret of Chloe's paternity was, it was this that was tearing him apart. And that on some level he was prepared for her to condemn him—because he had condemned himself.

"A human one," she said with all the conviction in her heart. "With normal feelings, normal reactions, trying to cope with a terribly abnormal situation. I'm not trying to tell you that how you feel doesn't matter, Shane, but it's what you *did* that's really important—and that was to do the best for your child under very trying circumstances. Don't you see? Despite everything, despite your own pain, you didn't repudiate Chloe, or blame her, or give her to somebody else to raise. Instead you put her needs above your own. You protected her and looked after her the best you could, and that's the true measure of being a parent. It doesn't matter who provided the sperm—*you're* Chloe's father."

He managed a shaky smile. "Yeah. I think I know that now. Watching you with her this summer, seeing you come to love her…it made me think. And then this weekend, when you were gone, I really missed her and I realized that lately I've stopped thinking about everything else. Chloe is just…Chloe. My daughter."

This time when she moved forward and put her arms around him, he didn't step away. "I'm so glad. So glad."

They stood silently for a good long while, just holding each other.

Finally Jessy leaned back. "I guess this explains why you're not real big on commitment," she said, conjuring up a smile. This, at least, was something she could make easy for him. "And it's all right. I understand—"

"Shh." He pressed a finger to her mouth. "There are a few more things I need to tell you."

"There are?"

"Yeah." Shane took a slow look around, seeing past the disorder to the splashes of color, the touches of warmth that Jessy had brought to the room. Like it, he'd been cold and empty before she'd come along. And now, thanks to her, he wasn't. "I don't want you to move out. Not when school starts. Not ever. Chloe loves you and needs a mother. And I need you—with me—forever."

"Please. You don't have to say this—"

"I love you, Jess. Part of me has loved you from that first day we met, when you were such a sweet, funny little kid. But all of me loves you now. I know it won't always be easy, but I want us to be together.''

"I love you, too."

And then there was no more need for words as he took her in his arms and they sealed their future together with a kiss.

* * * * *

FOLLOW THAT BABY...

the fabulous cross-line series featuring the infamously wealthy Wentworth family...continues with:

THE DADDY AND THE BABY DOCTOR
by **Kristin Morgan**
(Romance, 11/98)

The search for the mysterious Sabrina Jensen pits a seasoned soldier—and single dad—against a tempting baby doctor who knows Sabrina's best-kept secret....

Available at your favorite retail outlet, only from

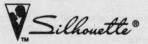

Take 2 bestselling love stories FREE

Plus get a FREE surprise gift!

Special Limited-Time Offer

Mail to Silhouette Reader Service™

3010 Walden Avenue
P.O. Box 1867
Buffalo, N.Y. 14240-1867

YES! Please send me 2 free Silhouette Desire® novels and my free surprise gift. Then send me 6 brand-new novels every month, which I will receive months before they appear in bookstores. Bill me at the low price of $3.12 each plus 25¢ delivery and applicable sales tax, if any.* That's the complete price, and a saving of over 10% off the cover prices—quite a bargain! I understand that accepting the books and gift places me under no obligation ever to buy any books. I can always return a shipment and cancel at any time. Even if I never buy another book from Silhouette, the 2 free books and the surprise gift are mine to keep forever.

225 SEN CH7U

Name	(PLEASE PRINT)
Address	Apt. No.
City	State Zip

This offer is limited to one order per household and not valid to present Silhouette Desire® subscribers. *Terms and prices are subject to change without notice.
Sales tax applicable in N.Y.

UDES-98   ©1990 Harlequin Enterprises Limited

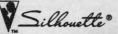

COMING NEXT MONTH

#1177 SLOW TALKIN' TEXAN—Mary Lynn Baxter
Ornery Porter Wyman, November's *Man of the Month*, was married to his Texas fortune, but money couldn't mother his baby boy. Sexy, nurturing Ellen Saxton...now, *she* could raise a child. *And* this single father's desire...for marriage?

#1178 HER HOLIDAY SECRET—Jennifer Greene
Her past twenty-four hours were a total blank! By helping elusive beauty Maggie Fletcher regain her lost day, small-town sheriff Andy Gautier was in danger of losing his *bachelorhood*. But would Maggie's holiday secret prevent her from becoming this lawman's Christmas bride?

#1179 THIRTY-DAY FIANCÉ—Leanne Banks
The Rulebreakers

Tough-as-nails Nick Nolan was lovely Olivia Polnecek's childhood protector. Now *she* was coming to *his* rescue by posing as his fiancée. She'd always dreamed of wearing Nick's ring, sleeping in his arms. So playing "devoted" was easy—and all part of her plan to turn their thirty-day engagement into a thirty-*year* marriage....

#1180 THE OLDEST LIVING MARRIED VIRGIN—
Maureen Child
The Bachelor Battalion

When innocent Donna Candello was caught tangled in Jack Harris's bedsheets, the honorable marine married her in name only. But their compromising position hadn't actually *compromised* Donna Candello at all...and the oldest living married virgin's first wedded task was to convince her new husband to give his blushing bride somethin' to *blush* about!

#1181 THE RE-ENLISTED GROOM—Amy J. Fetzer
Seven years ago levelheaded Maxie Parrish shocked rough-'n'-reckless Sergeant Kyle Hayden, leaving *him* at the altar. And nine months later Maxie had a surprise of her own! Now a certain never-forgotten ex-fiancé appeared at Maxie's ranch rarin' to round up the wife that got away...but what of the daughter he never knew?

#1182 THE FORBIDDEN BRIDE-TO-BE—Kathryn Taylor
Handsome, wealthy Alex Sinclair was Sophie Anders's perfect marriage match. Problem was, she already had a fiancé—his brother! True, her engagement was a phony, but the baby she was carrying was for real—and belonged to Alex. Once Sophie began to "show," would Alex make their forbidden affair into a wedded forever after?